WEIRD RULES
TO FOLLOW

WEIRD RULES TO FOLLOW

KIM SPENCER

ORCA BOOK PUBLISHERS

Published in Canada and the United States in 2022 by Orca Book Publishers.
orcabook.com

Library and Archives Canada Cataloguing in Publication
Title: Weird rules to follow / Kim Spencer.
Names: Spencer, Kim, author.
Identifiers: Canadiana (print) 20210381922 |
Canadiana (ebook) 20210381973 | ISBN 9781459835580 (softcover) |
ISBN 9781459835597 (PDF) | ISBN 9781459835603 (EPUB)
Classification: LCC PS8637.P4735 W45 2022 | DDC jC813/.6—dc23

Library of Congress Control Number: 2021951896

Summary: In this novel for middle readers told in vignettes,
Mia and her best friend, Lara, have very different experiences
growing up in a northern fishing community in the 1980s.

Orca Book Publishers is committed to reducing the consumption of
nonrenewable resources in the production of our books. We make
every effort to use materials that support a sustainable future.

Orca Book Publishers gratefully acknowledges the support for its publishing
programs provided by the following agencies: the Government of Canada,
the Canada Council for the Arts and the Province of British Columbia
through the BC Arts Council and the Book Publishing Tax Credit.

Cover artwork by Brayden Sato
Cover design by Dahlia Yuen
Interior design by Sydney Barnes
Edited by Jackie Lever and Tanya Trafford
Author photo by Belle Ancell

Printed and bound in Canada.

25   24   23   22 • 1   2   3   4

For my grandmother, mother and daughter.

Salmon Season, 1985

Prince Rupert is well known for rain and fishing. I've never known anything but. Like rain, salmon has always been a part of my life—in the ocean, on the stove, in the refrigerator or in my belly.

Most people say they like summer for the sun, but for coastal Natives, summer means one thing—salmon. The sockeye salmon season. It's an important time of year because that is how most Native people earn their living. It's also when we preserve our food for the winter.

Our small town begins stirring with excitement as Native people from surrounding villages arrive. Third Avenue bustles with cars and people. The adults seem happier when they are busy and there's work to do. The men go out commercial fishing, and the women (my mom and aunties included) put in long, hard hours at the fish cannery, which runs shifts around the clock.

It's the middle of summer. I go to visit my mom at the cannery on her lunch break, and even though we are outside, the smell of raw fish is everywhere. I wrinkle my nose. "Ewww, it smells."

My mom corrects me. "That's the smell of money."

And there is money to be made, all right.

Last payday, half the cannery workers got paid for overtime work, and there was a closure for fishing after an exceptionally good run, which meant fishermen received advances as well—the banks in Prince Rupert *ran out of money.* All of them. Everyone in town was talking about it.

When my mom and I were walking down Third Avenue that day, we bumped into someone she knew.

"Did you hear about the banks?" they asked. "Were you able to cash your check?"

Thankfully, she had cashed it.

I notice adults often carry fifty- or hundred-dollar bills during the summer months, and you can tell it makes them feel good. Those rich brown and vibrant red bills are commonplace.

We preserve our salmon in the summer. Food fish, the adults call it. It's a staple item that sustains us throughout the long winter months. Grandma always prepares ahead, well before she even gets fish. She gathers jars together to clean and then counts how many empty cases she has. If she happens to be short, she goes searching in our basement for more jars.

This is an adventure in itself, as you have to go outside, and the stairs leading down to our unfinished basement are overgrown with grass and a buildup of slippery moss.

Grandma is older and a bit heavier, and it shows in her movements. None of that deters her. Housedress and slippers on, she makes her way down there.

I follow along, as I know she needs the help. This time, the trek is worth it. "Ooh," Grandma says, as her eyes shimmer at all the jars she finds. That's mostly how she communicates—through her eyes.

Several of my cousins are at our house at any given time in the summer, while their parents are at work at the cannery. They've followed us to the basement and have gathered at the door. This pleases Grandma, as extra hands are always welcome. She starts to pass the Mason jars over to us grandkids one by one, and like an assembly line of little ants, we make our way back upstairs.

When someone from our reserve drops off a catch of sockeye salmon, Grandma is ready. She turns the kitchen table into a makeshift workstation by covering it with a flattened cardboard box.

Grandma is strong and has big arms and hands, but I can see removing the fish heads, then gutting and cleaning the fish isn't an easy job.

I stand quietly observing, being sure not to get in the way.

The fish heads go to one pile, and if there are eggs inside, they go to another. Then she cuts the fish into even smaller sections, holding up a slab of salmon against a pint or quart jar, making sure the cut is the right size.

This time she lets me measure and pour the salt into jars. This is an important job, as the amounts have to be exact.

Then she wipes down the mouth of the jars, fastens the lids, and into the boiler they go.

Grandma keeps the fish heads for baking—she never throws them out. "Don't waste seafood," she often says to me.

I'm used to her saying things like that. There are so many rules around not misusing or wasting our traditional foods.

The two of us eat the fish heads as an afternoon snack. My cousins would sooner play outside than eat fish heads. We don't mind, more for us!

I sit at the kitchen table watching closely as Grandma pulls the baking pan out of the oven and carefully places it on the table. There are almost a dozen salmon heads on the thin pan. I stare at them curiously. Their eyes slightly bulged from the heat, their tiny little sharp teeth still intact. I reach out to try and touch one of them.

Grandma reprimands me. "Don't play with the fish."

I think the fish heads are the best part of the salmon, very different from the rest. The meat inside is oily, and the texture silky-smooth. The only thing they need is a bit of salt. Grandma and I sit in our small kitchen not saying a word, eating our tasty fish heads until the meat of every last one of them is gone.

Grandma sets fish steaks aside to cook for dinner as well. I often hear adults say, "Fried fish is best when it's fresh!" She coats the fish in flour and then fries the steaks in a cast-iron pan and serves it with white rice and store-bought sweet pickles on the side.

When my mom and aunties walk in the door, they can tell by the smell that they're in for a delicious meal. Work uniform and kerchief still on, my mom digs in. "Luk'wil ts'imaatk," she says.

It *is* very tasty. I don't like the skin, though. I peel mine off with my fork, hold it up and ask, "Who wants my skin?"

My mom holds her plate toward me. I drop the piece of skin on it and she says, "That's the best part."

Grandma often shares fish with our non-Native neighbors as well. It's probably her way of saying thank you to them for mowing our lawn. They don't offer or ask to mow it—they just do it. After dinner, she asks me to go see if our neighbor could meet her at the fence between our houses.

My grandma mostly speaks in our Sm'algyax language, so when the father of the family next door reaches what's remaining of our fence, they don't say much. Grandma smiles with her eyes, he smiles and nods in return, and reaches over the fence to accept the big silvery sockeye from her.

Words aren't necessary. The language of sharing salmon is simple.

Pepto-Bismol

My name is Amelia Douglas. But everyone calls me Mia. My younger cousin Carmen couldn't pronounce my name when she was little; that's where Mia came in. I'm mostly called Amelia when I'm trouble. Grandma will say, "You're a bad girl, Amelia."

My mom and I live with my grandmother in her home. My grandfather bought the house before he passed away from cancer. I was only two when he died, so I have no memory of him. My mom's younger brother, Dan, and a foster girl named Mary live here as well.

Mary is five years older than I am and mostly thinks I'm a brat. I guess most of the time I am. Uncle Dan isn't that friendly, but we don't see him much. He's always in his room drinking beer and listening to music.

Our home is a hub for our large extended family. Different family members are always coming and going— aunts, uncles and cousins—like a continually revolving door. At least, that's how my mom refers to it. They move in if they happen to fall on hard times, then move out once they're able to get back on their feet.

Our door is never locked to anyone—literally. We don't have a key. We've never had one that I've known of. No one seems too concerned about it, though, or is in a hurry to get a new one.

I don't have a dad. No one talks about that, not ever. My mom has never said a word about him, and I don't ask.

Once, in a teasing way, Grandma asked me who my dad was. It hurt my feelings that she asked that. Like she was making fun of me.

I know she didn't mean anything by it, because she never upsets me like that. If something makes me sad, my tummy will start to ache. I don't know why this happens, but Grandma's the one who usually makes me feel better. I go and sit on her lap or lean into her and it goes away.

When she isn't around, I usually reach for the Pepto-Bismol. Well, that was until my cousin Tonya laughed at me when I asked for some the other day. She said she'd never heard a kid ask for Pepto-Bismol before.

Summer Fish and Chips

It's Saturday, and the sun is out. My best friend and I make the most of the day by playing on the street in front of my home.

Lara is Mexican Hungarian. I'm mostly Native Indian. I say "mostly" because my skin is lighter brown. Some people think that we look alike. I guess we have similarities, like dark brown hair. But I'm a slimmer build and a bit darker-skinned than she is.

We've both recently turned ten years old and have lived on the same cul-de-sac, four houses apart, to be exact, for as long as we can remember. Lara lives in a large white house at the end of the street. They have a view of the mountains and the ocean and they overlook town. Her family has two cars in the driveway, two living rooms, two fireplaces, two bathrooms and a laundry room. It's one of the nicest houses on our street, and the kind of home people like me can only dream about. Our home is an old wartime house, our view is a retaining wall, and there is no car parked out front. It has original everything, at a time when original has no value. Our bathroom has an old claw-foot tub. We have no washer and dryer or dishwasher, and the kitchen appliances are all mismatched. Lara lives with her parents and little brother, Owen. Her mom is strict, so she isn't usually allowed to go to other people's houses. But I'm always welcome at their place, to play after school, for meals or for weekend sleepovers. One of the first times I remember going to Lara's house was when I was around six years old. Lara and I were taking our shoes off at the door. Her mom was sitting on the living room sofa, and without taking her eyes off the television she said, "Your friend's not going to say hello?"

It seemed like an order rather than a suggestion.

I didn't know you were supposed to greet your friend's parents when you entered their home.

"Hi," I said shyly, like I'd just forgotten to say it. After that, I made sure to say hello every time I entered their place.

I know there will be no one home at my place this afternoon, which is why I decide to ask Lara if she'd like to come over for lunch. This is unusual, as we rarely hang out together at my house.

My friend eagerly accepts the invitation, and we make our way toward my place. When we go inside, I don't bother looking around to see if it's tidy. And I don't look to see Lara's reaction either. If she thinks my house is strange compared to her place, where the furniture all matches and there are actual doorknobs on the doors, she doesn't mention it.

For lunch I decide to make us fish and chips. I often watch my older cousin Al fry dollar chips. I guess I must have been paying close attention because even though I have never made them before, I know exactly what to do.

I grab a couple of russet potatoes, wash them and start slicing them into dollar chips. I place the cast-iron pan on the stove and heat the oil. I cautiously place the potato pieces into the pan, let them fry and then carefully turn them over, just like I've seen Al do. Once they're the perfect golden color, I remove them from the pan.

All the while, Lara stands there with a look of wonder. I don't know if it's because of my newfound cooking skills or seeing my home for the first time. Lara tends to do this thing where she averts her eyes from me if something's awkward or embarrassing so I don't feel uncomfortable. I think she's doing it now in not looking around our messy kitchen.

I know our house is different. Our cupboard doors no longer close properly after Al painted them yellow. But now isn't the time to worry about that.

When the dollar chips are done, I set them aside and go to open a quart jar of salmon. I spoon some out onto our plates and then add the potatoes. "Fish and chips," I proudly exclaim.

We eat our lunch at the kitchen table. We lightly salt our chips and add some ketchup on the side. We barely speak, but that isn't important. What matters is, I'm hosting lunch and for the first time ever my best friend is a welcomed guest in my home. We've forgotten the other kids we left playing on the street and that the sun is still shining. Visiting at my home is new to us and feels long overdue. The freedom we feel is everything.

That freedom doesn't last. Lara's little brother, Owen, must have felt left out and tattled on us. When the telephone rings, we're surprised it's Lara's mother. The very thought of her daughter being at my home must have made her uneasy. However, she says she's calling to invite us to join her and Owen at a popular fish and chips place. "No thanks," Lara says matter-of-factly. "Mia just made us fish and chips."

But her mother insists we join them. We find ourselves standing at the Green Apple counter. Lara objects again. "We're not hungry, *we just ate fish and chips*, remember?" To satisfy her mom and the person patiently waiting to take our order, we both ask for chocolate milk.

The restaurant is nearly empty, so we choose a seat by the window. We settle in. No one says anything and it feels awkward. Lara's mom looks across the table at us and forces a half smile to her face that fades just as quickly. I'm uncomfortable around her most of the time, but today, even more so. I can't tell if she's upset that I cooked for her daughter or that I had the nerve to have her in my home. I do my best to avoid her gaze.

Her mom eventually breaks the silence by asking me how I made my fish and chips.

In a shy yet proud way, I start to share my recipe with her, explaining the intricate methods of frying like I'd been doing it for years.

She interrupts me. "What kind of fish did you use?"

I vaguely describe the fish to her—I mean, it's fish. What more can I say?

She continues to prod. "Was it halibut or salmon?"

Now I know what she's getting at.

I want her to know that it wasn't just any kind of canned fish I'd served. "It was a jar of sockeye salmon my grandma made."

Lara's mom suddenly loses interest. She turns away muttering, "That's not real fish and chips."

The table goes back to silence.

I want to defend my recipe, but I don't know how or what I would even say. Lara regularly defends herself to others, but I don't. Native kids aren't like that. I try to sit as tall as I can in my chair, though, so it's clear I am standing by my version of fish and chips despite being told it's not "real."

When the food finally arrives, Lara's mom examines her meal and looks pleased with the golden stack of fries and crispy pieces of fish in front of her. She offers to share some of her fish and chips with us.

Lara refuses. "Mia's was better."

I don't know if she means it, as she'd hardly touched any of the food I'd made earlier. Either way, I appreciate the support.

Her mom looks at me, waiting for a reply.

Still sitting tall, I shake my head. "No, thank you."

The enjoyment from our earlier lunch is long gone, seeped like air from a balloon. I look out the restaurant window. I try to ignore the mouthwatering smells of deep-fried food while struggling to make sense of things. I knew my recipe was different. I've had this kind before too. I just don't understand why my first attempt at cooking fish and chips was turned into a competition.

The Tooth Fairy

Owen lost his front tooth last night. He's so cute—he makes a whistling sound when he speaks now.

His parents put a one-dollar bill under his pillow. He's been dangling it in our faces, showing off, while Lara and I play Barbies.

Lara acknowledges his presence by squeezing Owen's cheeks together and saying, "Look at that cute face!"

She's rarely that nice to him.

If he only knew how much I got for a tooth once, he certainly wouldn't be bragging.

We were on a weekend getaway to Terrace with my family. I was the only kid with them that time, which wasn't unusual. Most of my cousins are older than me and often have the option to stay home. I was only eight.

We had grabbed dinner at Shan-Yan's, the local Chinese food place, and then headed back to the Slumber Lodge Motel, where we'd already checked in.

My mom, Aunt Lorraine, Uncle Jerry and I shared a room. My cousin Al, his wife Yolanda and Uncle Dan were staying in an adjoining room. We left the doors between the rooms open while we visited.

They settled in and opened beers that had been chilling in the bathtub they'd filled with ice from the vending machine.

"Why didn't we stay at the Sandman?" I asked. "I could've gone swimming. Now what am I supposed to do all night?"

"It was sold out," Uncle Jerry answered.

"Where are the books you brought?" my mom asked.

I sighed, hung my shoulders and walked to the other room to get them out of my overnight bag. My front tooth was loose and had been bugging me for a few days. I worked at loosening it further with my tongue as I searched through my bag. Suddenly, the tooth fell out.

No matter how much you're expecting it, even when you're trying to loosen it, having your tooth fall out is a surprise.

"I lost my tooth!" I yelled, as I walked back to the other room.

"Let me see," my mom said.

"Hoh jeh," Al said, examining the tooth in my hand carefully. "A front tooth. I bet you'll get lots of money for that one."

I flashed him a grin and walked around the room, palm open, proudly showing everyone. Then I put it in my jean pocket for safekeeping.

"Will the tooth fairy be able to find you at a hotel?" Uncle Jerry asked with a serious face, even though he was only teasing. "How will she know what room you're in?"

Aunt Lorraine waved at him with a dismissive hand. "Let me look," she said. She meant the gap in my mouth.

I went and stood in front of her and opened my mouth wide.

"Ḵ'as'waan," she teased, tickling my tummy. That means "toothless" in our language.

I spent the evening rereading *Frog and Toad*, my tongue unable to resist playing with the new space in my mouth. I had picked the book up at our school's book fair and had read it so many times already. " 'Blah,' said Toad." Bored, I closed the book and went and asked the adults for change for the vending machine to get snacks.

Everyone started digging around in their pockets for loose change. They're always generous when they're drinking.

I walked to the vending machine at the end of the hall. I had enough money for a pop, a bag of chips and a chocolate bar. I put the exact change in, chose my item and stood staring at the machine as it slowly turned and dropped the bag of chips. I did the same for my chocolate bar. There's always a chance they'll get stuck in the machine, so you can't take your eyes off them for a second.

When I couldn't stay awake a minute longer, I said good night to everyone. They were all in a good mood and laughing.

I went to lie on our hotel bed. I was so tired I didn't bother changing into my pyjamas. I started thinking about things.

When adults drink too much they tend to get clumsy and forget things or don't make any sense when they speak. I'd lost my tooth a few hours ago. That was many beers ago. There was no way any of them would remember.

I took my tooth out of my pocket, examined it and then carefully placed it under the hotel pillow. If there's really such a thing as a tooth fairy, I thought to myself, she'll find me at the hotel. If there is money under my pillow tomorrow, I'll know for sure she's real.

I woke late the next morning. Everyone else was already awake. I sat up, taking a moment to remember where we were, and then wondered what time it was.

The smell of stale beer and leftover Chinese food lingered in the room. The orange-and-brown curtains were slightly opened, and the sun was peeking through, which made me glad. It didn't rain in Terrace as much as it did in Rupert.

"Good morning, sleepyhead." Aunty Lorraine said, smiling.

"Morning," I mumbled while stretching.

Then I remembered my tooth. I turned and slowly lifted my pillow. My tooth was gone and staring back at me was a twenty-dollar bill!

I stared, stunned. I'd never gotten that much money for a tooth before. I reached for the crisp bill.

"Whoa, look who's rich! The tooth fairy left you lots of money!" Uncle Jerry exclaimed.

Beaming, I flashed him a big grin and continued examining the sheen on the green bill.

"I guess you're buying breakfast?" he added with a laugh.

Aunt Lorraine waved him away again.

He always likes to kid around like that.

That's right. I got a *twenty-dollar bill* for my lost tooth. I'd never tell Owen that, of course.

Must Have Been the Indians

Our cul-de-sac sits above a hill. Cars or people that aren't supposed to be there are rare.

When we are playing on the road and cars we don't recognize drive through, we clear off to the side. Our eyes stay on the vehicle the whole time. It's more out of curiosity, but we must look like neighborhood watchdogs.

Lara has the best bike. It's teal green, with a sparkly white banana seat. It has chopper-style handlebars, with green and white tassels hanging from them. The most fun feature is that not only can two people fit on the seat, but a third person fits on the handlebars!

When we're bored and feel like being nice to Owen, we invite him to join us. The three of us race to the end of the street, Lara steering, her little brother settled in front of her, and me on the handlebars. Then we make our way back, happily coasting until the bike comes to a stop.

We've enjoyed many fun-filled summers doubling up and down our street on her bike. Where my friend goes, I go.

This afternoon, though, for no apparent reason, Lara suddenly steers out of control and we crash.

"I farted!" Lara shrieks. She starts laughing uncontrollably. "When we fell, I farted!"

Since I was the one thrown from the handlebars, I feel a bit shaken. I get up, brush myself off and check my knees and elbows for any scrapes. Relieved there are none.

I glare at Lara. How could she be so careless?

She doesn't even notice. She's still laughing, pinned beneath the bike.

I lean over and lift the bike off her, and in my sternest voice say, "From now on, I'm driving."

She laughs even more.

The next week, when Lara, Owen and I get back to Lara's place after swimming at the pool, her father tells us that both Lara's and Owen's bikes have been stolen.

None of us say a word.

Who would do such a thing?

Even though I have my own bike, Lara's banana-seat bike feels like my bike—I feel the loss as much as she does.

I wonder if one of the kids on our street borrowed the bikes but forgot to return them.

As if reading my mind, her father says, "I walked the entire street, looking into people's yards for the bikes. They are nowhere to be found."

It starts to sink in—the bikes are gone. We stand in the driveway stunned, backpacks hanging.

Lara's father stares out into nothing, distant-like. "Someone stole the kids' bikes…" he says, maybe to himself.

Then he turns his attention back to us and adds, "It must have been the Indians."

He looks at me and gives me a wink.

I don't react. And I don't look to see what Lara's reaction is either.

I am too ashamed.

I know I am Indian, but Lara and I have never talked about that kind of stuff before.

And I also know stealing is wrong. And that Lara's dad has just accused Indians, us, of stealing the bikes, even though he has no way of knowing for sure.

His words hang in the air.

Suddenly I am the one staring out into nothing, distant-like. Except I am only pretending, pretending I didn't hear those words.

Whoever Needs Healing

On the weekends, if there's nothing good to watch on TV, I go to church with Grandma.

She attends wherever the Natives congregate. It's either the Native Pentecostal or some other nondenominational group that has formed. Right now it's a place called the Upper Room.

They change every few years, depending on church funds or the number of steady followers. Sometimes it's because a church leader is backsliding.

I had to ask my mom what backsliding meant. She says it means they've either gone back to drinking or playing bingo.

I am not a regular churchgoer and don't consider myself Christian, but Grandma always extends the invitation.

"Are you coming to church tonight?" she asks.

"Are they serving cake?" I reply.

Grandma's eyes gleam as she laughs. "Hoogxh, you don't just go to church for the cake!"

We are sitting in the audience. I'm used to the preacher's style of teaching hellfire. He yells into the microphone now and again, sprays of spit flying, delivering a strong message of damnation to partygoers and bingo players alike.

I remember one time we were at a memorial service, and the preacher said the only reason people were there instead of at bingo was because someone had died. My mom and her sisters, who play bingo regularly, were furious.

At the end of the sermon tonight, the preacher calls out for anyone who needs healing to come stand in front of the altar.

Grandma motions me to get up. I follow her lead, as I have done many times before.

The preacher is making his way through the crowd that has already formed, his long microphone cord snaking its way behind him. He asks each person what is troubling them and proceeds to pray (holler) into the microphone as his right hand rests on top of their head to bless them.

When it's our turn, Grandma makes me stand in front of her, her hands resting on my shoulders. Grandma's tall, almost as tall as the preacher. She leans in toward him like it's important he listen closely to what she's about to say.

"Can you pray for my granddaughter? Her mom's an alcoholic."

I can't believe my ears.

You don't talk about those kinds of things! Let alone tell it to the guy who's about to yell for the entire room to hear.

I have no time to process what is happening. The preacher's hand is now on my head, pressing harder and harder with each "In the name of Jesus!"

It feels like *I* am the alcoholic. And the man is attempting to knock it out of my system.

I've never felt so angry. My grandmother broke the number one rule. You don't talk openly about shameful things like that. You hide them. How could she not know this?

When what feels like an exorcism rather than a prayer is over, I go and sit back in my seat and angrily cross both arms tightly over my chest.

Dark Skin and Slim Waists

We've had a lot of sun this summer, so I'm super tanned. Of course, Uncle Dan called me Mowgli again the other day.

Last Christmas, Uncle Ted and Aunty Becky took me to Hawaii for a couple of weeks with their kids, Tonya and David. I got so tanned!

When we came back, Uncle Dan saw me, laughed and said, "Now Mia really looks like Mowgli."

I was tired of him saying that all the time, so I asked my mom, "Why does he call me that?"

"It's a character from *The Jungle Book*. Haven't you seen it?"

"No." I shook my head.

"It's an old one. The boy is skinny, has dark skin and short hair, just like you!"

I didn't appreciate my uncle saying I looked like a boy. But I agree, when I have lots of sun, my skin gets pretty darn dark.

Lara is by no means fat, but her mother always has her on a diet. Probably because she's always dieting too, weighing her chicken breasts on a scale and stuff. She even makes Lara drink skim milk, which is just gross. It's like dunking your cookies into cloudy water.

We're playing Barbies in Lara's room when her mom comes in and says something to her in Spanish.

Lara argues back in English.

I'm used to them talking like that. I pretend not to notice.

Her mom snaps at her once again.

And Lara lifts her shirt, revealing a thick belt wrapped around her waist.

I sneak a peek while making like Barbie is walking to her car. The belt looks like it's from her karate uniform and is tightly wrapped around her waist several times. Barbie has reached her destination, but I'm still making walking motions.

Lara's mom appears satisfied and leaves the room.

"What is that for?" I ask quietly as Lara pulls her shirt back down.

"I don't want to talk about it," she mutters.

I go home and tell my mom about Lara's strange belt. She already knows about the skimmed milk. She says it's weird for a kid to be on a diet (my mom tries to diet too, and likes to drink Fresca or Tab).

My mom looks surprised. "It's what women used to do in the olden days to make their waists smaller."

I don't question it further. Or ask whether I should be concerned about having a small waist too.

Those People

It's payday Friday, and the sun is out. We're nearing the end of summer and fishing is starting to slow. My family finally got a day off work, so we are on our way to Terrace for a weekend getaway. The adults sip on their cold beers, and us kids are eating junk food we purchased at the corner store.

My mom doesn't drive or own a car. We usually travel with Aunt Lorraine, Uncle Jerry and their three kids, Sherrie, Susan and Travis. We can all easily cram into one vehicle.

Aunt Lorraine's in a good mood. She's dancing with her shoulders, holding an unlit cigarette in her left hand. "Light me, Jerry!" she belts out.

Uncle Jerry pushes the car lighter in, and when it pops out again he holds it up. Aunt Lorraine leans toward him, still shimming her shoulders, and inhales.

Uncle Jerry's in a country-music phase right now. Mel Tillis's "Coca-Cola Cowboy" is playing on the cassette.

We come across highway construction. My uncle slows the vehicle and turns the music down.

A blond guy wearing a hard hat and holding a stop sign approaches the vehicle. His eyes are aqua blue.

"Delay shouldn't be too long," he informs us.

The flagger and my uncle start making small talk.

My mom's sitting in the seat behind Aunt Lorraine. They're probably the closest amongst all the sisters. They are looking toward the Skeena River, whispering back and forth.

I don't pay attention to what they're saying. Susan and I are trading some of our candies in the back seat. I want to make sure I'm getting a good deal because my older cousins like to pull fast ones on me.

As Uncle Jerry's chatting with the flagger, he reaches behind his seat and pulls a cold can of beer from a small cooler. He hands it to the flagger and says, "For your break."

A grin spreads across the blond guy's face. "Thanks," he says as he puts the can in the back pocket of his faded jeans.

It always surprises me that *those* people like beer too.

I thought mostly Natives did. I know my family drinks a lot of it. I also wonder why the flagger isn't hiding the beer. Shouldn't he be embarrassed about it?

When traffic is allowed to proceed, we continue slowly, and then begin picking up speed. I move up to the middle of the front seat. I rewind the song to the beginning and adjust the volume. Once again we're on our way, the mighty Skeena to our right and Mel Tillis in our hearts.

Hospital Corners

Lara and I never get bored when we hang out. We can play for hours and hours and never notice how much time has passed. I forget about things like my mom's drinking, or that there are so many people living in our house with us. Lara's home is like an escape—well, for me anyway.

Lara's bedroom is mostly pink, from the sheer drapes to the plush dusty-rose carpet. Even the wallpaper is light pink and gray. Her furniture is all white and matches. The pleats on her bedspread reach to the floor and her pillows tuck under like in a hotel room. It's the most beautiful room I've ever seen, just like the one you'd see in the movies.

She has a system for getting ready for bed each night. She doesn't use the bedspread or extra pillow because they're "decorative." And in the morning, it's a whole other system for making the bed. The corners of the top sheet have to be done in a specific fold. She also showed me the trick to the fancy hotel pillow. It's so easy.

When I sleep over, if Lara leaves her bed unmade for too long, her mom will remind her to make it. She does both routines every single day.

After the first sleepover at her place, I went home and told my mom about Lara's bed-making ritual and the specific way she folds her sheets. My mom stared at me for a moment and then said, "Hospital corners. Her mom must have worked at a hospital or as a maid."

Don't Marry an Indian

Bob Seger's hit song "Old Time Rock and Roll" is echoing from the stereo inside the house.

We can hear someone singing along to the chorus, getting right into it. Words slower, but not quite slurring. Our family tends to get louder the more they drink. Happier.

My cousin Michael and I are in the backyard at his older sister Patti's home. We're sitting on top of a picnic table—it's an unusually warm September evening for Rupert. We ordered pizza and just finished eating.

"That was delicious," I say.

"It was," Michael replies as he throws his pizza crust into the empty box.

I have just started fifth grade. Michael's in eighth grade. He's suddenly acting so cool because he's in junior high now.

Michael's half-Native, the same as me, but his skin is much lighter than mine. He's been carrying on about all the pretty white girls at school for an hour. I'm half listening to him, half straining to hear our family inside.

I think I prefer non-junior-high Michael better. At least then we weren't talking about girls all the time. We used to play video games, swing on the monkey bars and ride our bikes. That reminds me of one disastrous time we'd gone out biking.

I'd just gotten a new BMX bike, and he challenged me to race around the block. I was winning. He was so close to catching up but couldn't. We were angling a curve at the bottom of the hill when he yelled out, "You know there are no brakes on that bike, right?"

I had been pedaling as fast as I could when I heard what Michael said. *No brakes?* I leapt from my bike and went flying through the air. I landed on the ground, my right shoulder dragging on the cement until I came to a stop.

When I looked up, Michael was staring down at me, still on his bike. He looked like he was going to cry. "I'm going to get help," he said and then rode off.

I'd stayed there motionless, in shock. I don't know why hearing "no brakes" made me panic like that. I've been riding bikes since my first tricycle. I know exactly how they work—bikes eventually slow if you stop pedaling.

I start rubbing the scar on my right shoulder from that day. Michael is still talking about pretty white girls.

"My mom told me not to marry an Indian."

His words take me by surprise. And confuse me. His mom, my aunt, *is* Indian. Why would she say something like that to him?

I like white boys as much as the next girl. In fact, I've developed a new crush on a white boy in my class named Todd. I sharpen my pencil more than usual because his desk is right beside the sharpener.

Still, I don't know how to respond. "Hmm," I say. "It's getting cold." Then I add, "Maybe we should head back inside."

But my aunt's words stay with me. Sting like a betrayal. Is there something wrong with us?

Bingo!

When my mom arrives home from bingo night, the first thing I ask is if she won. The answer is usually no.

Once in a while she wins fifty or one hundred dollars. It's always a mystery—I never know what she'll say.

"Did you win?" I ask, looking up from the TV as my mom walks through the door this evening.

"The jackpot!" she says, waving a thick wad of money back and forth.

That's the final game of the night. They pay out cash prizes, so it's a lot of money she's flashing about.

I leap off the couch and jump around excited in front of her. "How much, how much?!"

"A thousand dollars," she replies happily.

"A THOUSAND DOLLARS?" I repeat. "Yahoo!" I dance around the living room.

Mary's smiling, but mostly at my dancing. Grandma's sitting in her armchair and has that sparkly look she gets in her eyes when she's happy.

Even though it's after ten, we order pizza.

My mom, Grandma, Mary and I eat while watching old reruns. Uncle Dan comes down from his room and grabs a few slices and goes back upstairs. He never joins us for meals, unless it's a holiday or special occasion.

The next day I go to Lara's. We're standing in her dining room when I tell her about my mom winning the night before. Her mouth hangs open.

"My mom's taking me shopping this afternoon and then we're going for dinner at Rodhos," I tell her. It's a nice feeling having all this extra money.

Just then Lara's mom enters the room. "Hi, Mia. What were you saying about bingo?"

"My mom won a thousand dollars last night!" I smile proudly.

"But how much money did she have to spend to *get* that thousand dollars?" Lara's mom asks, her eyes piercing through me like lasers.

I don't understand what she means, but her tone makes me shrink a little inside.

She continues, "How many nights a week does she go to bingo? She probably spends, what, thirty or fifty dollars? But she doesn't win any of those times, does she? Don't you see? She's just getting her money back, and not even as much as she originally spent."

I nod my head. I don't know how else to reply. Winning the jackpot suddenly doesn't seem exciting.

Lara's mom is carrying on about gambling now. I've heard the word before. I'm no longer listening, though; just nodding now and again.

I wish I'd never brought it up. Lara was excited for me a few minutes earlier; now she's staring out the window.

We go shopping and then out for dinner. Rodhos is small and cozy. It has wooden arches, decorative wool rugs on the walls, and tables covered by blue-and-white-checkered tablecloths. We eat here often in the summer on my mom's paydays. It's delicious.

My shopping bags are piled on a seat at the table like a third dinner guest. I bought two new outfits and a pair of LA Gear runners that I've wanted for a while. We also went to the bookstore and my mom let me buy two Sweet Valley High books.

My mom orders a steak and tells me to get one as well, but I like their baked lasagne with meatballs. When we go out to dinner with other adults, they sometimes enjoy beer or wine with their meal, but my mom never orders alcoholic drinks when it's just the two of us.

While we wait for our food, I think about telling my mom what Lara's mom said. I don't want to upset her, but I'm curious to know what she thinks of gambling. I'm tracing a line on the tablecloth with my index finger. I look up, act casual and then tell her everything Lara's mom said.

My mom's sitting across from me, listening closely. When I'm done, she rolls her eyes and says, "I know how gambling works! But it's entertainment—I do it because it's fun."

I almost breathe a sigh of relief. I'm glad what Lara's mom said didn't affect her mood the way it had mine.

I picture my mom and her four sisters sitting in the bingo hall, drinking coffee and laughing, with their bingo cards and dabbers spread out before them—*having fun*.

Big Mom

Grandma is getting ready for church. She always fixes herself up nice and wears a dress and blazer whether she's going to church or the grocery store. She invites me to come along, but it's Thursday and there are always good shows on TV, so I don't go.

The Upper Room is one block from a district known as Bucket of Blood because a lot of drunken brawls have broken out there over the years. They say the district used to be called Apache Pass by white people, which the adults say is downright ignorant, as there are no Apache Indians in Prince Rupert or anywhere near it.

Two main bars in the district are located across the street from one another—the Belmont and the Empress. Over the weekend someone painted a diagonal sidewalk that went between the two bars, exactly where people jaywalk.

My mom and her siblings thought that was pretty funny. They weren't surprised when the City quickly painted over it first thing Monday.

My cousin Patti, Michael's older sister, is closer to my mom's age than mine. She always dresses glamorously when she goes out to bars. She wears revealing halter tops, gold sequin earrings and bright red lipstick.

She told me once that in between walking from bar to bar, she sometimes drops in at church to visit Big Mom (what my older cousins call our grandmother).

Grandma usually sits at the back of the church in an aisle seat. Patti says she quietly slips in, making sure her high heels don't clack too loudly on the floor. Noticeably dressed for a nightclub rather than church, she takes a seat next to Grandma.

The only communication they exchange is eye contact. But it is enough. Patti rests her head on Grandma's shoulder and basks in her calming energy and love, hoping for a hint of that goodness to rub off.

Then she squeezes Grandma's arm real tight and makes her way back to the bar scene.

Patti says Grandma has never judged or scolded her for showing up at church like that. She says it's Grandma's way of leaving the door to her faith open.

When I tell Patti about Grandma making me go to the altar to be prayed over, she laughs and says, "Big Mom does that to me too."

Raise Your Hand If You're Native Indian

Lara and I are in the same fifth-grade class. We made sure to sit next to each other on the first day, but the teacher quickly separated our desks for talking too much.

We are learning about explorers and fur traders in Social Studies. It used to be my favorite subject, but lately I'm finding these lessons boring.

There's going to be an assembly this afternoon. I look forward to them because it's a reason to get out of the classroom. Posters have been displayed around the school for a few weeks that say a Coast Salish dance group will be performing. We've never had Native dancers come to our school before.

When it's time for the assembly, the teacher tells us to line up at the door. I take my time putting my books away. I look up and see Lara frantically motioning me over to where she's standing.

I join her in line and at the same time we say, "We get to sit together!" and high-five each other with both hands.

Once we are settled in the gymnasium, the principal welcomes the dance group and then hands the mic over to one of the dancers.

"My name is Evan Adams," he says to the audience. "I am Coast Salish, and a member of the Sliammon Nation." He's wearing traditional regalia.

"How many of you in the audience are Native Indian? Please raise your hand."

Students at my school have never been asked that question before, not in class, let alone at a large assembly.

Quite a few kids all around me raise their hands.

They do it naturally, like it's a question they get asked every day.

And in front of white people.

I'm too embarrassed to raise my hand. But I feel equally ashamed for not raising it.

I glance sideways at Lara to see if she notices. She's staring at the speaker.

I quickly decide that if anyone asks why I didn't put my hand up, I will say I didn't hear the question.

I admire the Native students who put their hands up. They seem so comfortable with themselves. I can't imagine feeling that way.

The speaker continues, "It's nice to see so many of you in the audience. Always be proud of who you are, be proud of being Native Indian."

I feel even worse. Like I need some Pepto-Bismol.

Those Schools

A lot of kids live on our street. Most are Native like me. There's not a lot of change in the neighborhood, so it feels like we've all grown up together.

When we play outside, we never run out of things to do. There's skip rope, hopscotch, softball, soccer stop or a game called Dungeon.

For that game, we divide into two teams. The aim is to catch whoever isn't on your team, and when you do, you bring them to the dungeon. The dungeon is a large staircase landing enclosed by railings. The only way the person caught can be freed is if someone from their team tags them or when everyone on the opposing team is caught. Then we switch sides.

It's so much fun. Except we don't get to play it much because the family whose staircase landing is *the dungeon* is sometimes mean. The mom yells out the door at us. Sometimes we deserve it. Like when we sneak into their backyard and pick their blueberries and huckleberries. Other times, there's no good reason for it.

Like the incident that happened today. I complain to my mom when I get home, "Peter's mom yelled at us again. She's not that nice, you know—she can be really mean."

"She went to one of *those schools*," my mom says.

"What schools?"

"They used to take Native children away from their parents, force them to go to schools, and they didn't treat them good."

I don't understand what that has to do with Peter's mom being mean to us, but I don't ask any more questions.

Our Tears Are Different Than Their Tears

It never fails to amaze me how white girls can cry at the drop of a hat.

If someone looks at them wrong, they think the teacher is being unfair or another kid teases them, even a little, suddenly big fat tears are streaming down their faces.

It doesn't matter what the class is doing or who is there. They'll cry in front of our teacher, the principal or even a cute boy—none of that seems to matter to them.

I can't help but stare in wonder at their ability to turn on the waterworks as casually as one turns a tap on or off.

Today in the middle of math, a girl named Amanda walks away from the teacher's desk and starts crying in front of the entire fifth-grade class.

When the teacher asks her what's wrong, she doesn't respond. She just keeps on with the tears.

I watch her from my desk. I try to picture myself standing in front of our class. My eyes closed, lips curled downward into an exaggerated pout, crying my dark-brown eyes out.

I can't do it.

I can't even imagine I am doing it. Not even in my make-believe world can I dare be that free.

This ability to cry in public isn't the only thing that intrigues me about these girls. I'm also amazed by how little it takes to make them cry. *A boy called me a name, wah. So-and-so peeked at my test, wah. I got three answers wrong on my quiz, wah.*

By the time I got to fifth grade, I'd already seen so many dreadful, painful things—it took a lot for me to get upset. The things these girls cry about are ridiculous.

Native girls don't cry like the white girls do. One of the few times I saw a Native girl cry at school was in this same class, a few months back. April is a girl whose family is known for being poor. That day she was frantically waving her hand and asking permission to go to the washroom. It was obvious she was desperate.

The teacher denied her request.

A few minutes later there was a puddle on the floor under her desk. Some of the kids started to giggle.

I hated myself for it, but I did too. Actually, I laughed louder than I should have.

April sat staring straight ahead, her eyes on the chalkboard. A few tears rolled slowly down her face.

After the janitor cleaned the floor, I walked by April's desk and nodded at her, hoping to reassure her. She immediately looked away. I didn't blame her. I had behaved cruelly.

Our tears are different than their tears. White tears get a lot of sympathy and attention. They are like show-and-tell tears. Our tears, the few that are shed, seem to make people uncomfortable.

The first Native girl I ever saw cry was named Laurie. We were in third grade. She arrived late, and not just by a few minutes either. She had her little brother Christopher with her, her arm around him protectively. She walked with him to the front of the classroom and stood there until the teacher acknowledged her.

Our teacher, Mrs. Hoshino, was an older Japanese woman who smelled of mints. She looked irritated at the disruption. She glanced down at Laurie's brother, then asked Laurie where she had been. We hadn't seen her in class for quite a while.

"My mom and her boyfriend have been drinking, and he beat my mom up. We have no food and I have to look after my brother. That's why I haven't been able to come to school," Laurie stated.

The teacher grimaced slightly as she tried to make sense of what she'd just heard.

Mrs. Hoshino had recently taught us how to use an abacus. I imagined her sliding wooden beads back and forth, trying to find a solution to the brown-skinned kids that stood before her.

I guess she found the answer. "Go," she said, without any bit of sympathy, pointing toward the hallway with the piece of chalk she always had in her hand. "Go to the principal's office."

The image of Laurie and Christopher standing at the front of the class stayed with me for the rest of the afternoon. The sinking feeling I felt was worse than shame. We were eight years old. I wanted to whisper to Laurie to sit down and be quiet. I'd seen people drunk many times. I'd seen fights as well. I wanted to tell her she's not supposed to talk about those kinds of things. Yet at the same time, my heart ached for Laurie, who was trying so desperately to care for her little brother. Christopher was so cute too. He was in kindergarten and had wide brown eyes and big smooth cheeks you wanted to either squeeze or kiss.

I went home and told my mom what had happened with Laurie that day. She nodded at me, all serious, and then turned to my aunt. "I heard he went to one of *those schools*," she said. She was talking about the boyfriend. The one who'd beaten up Laurie's mother.

My mom's mentioned *those schools* before. It's weird how she always talks about them in low tones, like she doesn't want anyone to hear.

The Devil's Music

Lara is Catholic. I went to her church with her and her mom once. The service was held in a church that had high ceilings and large stained-glass windows.

It was very different from Grandma's church, which is held in an old carpet-and-tile store. And the service was in the morning, whereas Grandma's church is in the evening.

A man was dressed in a long ornate robe.

"Who's that guy supposed to be?" I whispered to Lara.

"He's the priest, the father."

I noticed he didn't raise his voice or yell like the preacher at Grandma's church did.

The pews were mostly empty that day, and the service brief. It definitely didn't have the same intensity as the Upper Room. It felt like we were at a funeral or something.

When it was over, the adults went down to the basement for coffee and cigarettes.

I'm playing at Lara's after school. We're in the den, listening to music on her father's eight-track player. It's old-fashioned, but we think it's cool.

The Supremes: Greatest Hits is our go-to album. We both agree "Where Did Our Love Go" is the best song ever.

An album in her father's music collection suddenly catches my eye. It's by a band named Kiss. I never noticed it before, but when I was at church with Grandma over the weekend the preacher mentioned this band—he said they played the devil's music.

I decide to share this important information with Lara.

She is hanging on my every word, her eyes getting wider and wider. Then I tell her the scariest part. "They say if you play it on a record player backward, it's the devil's voice."

"DADDY!" she screams, running out of the room.

I wasn't expecting that response.

At the bottom of the stairs, she calls out again for her father.

I follow closely behind.

The upstairs door opens. "What is all this ruckus?" her dad asks.

"You have to come down here right now," Lara insists.

He follows us into the den. "What is this all about, Lara?" he asks again.

Lara points to his eight-tracks on the shelf. "Mia says Kiss is the devil's music! Daddy, please get rid of it!"

The concerned look on her father's face disappears.

"Tell him, Mia!" Lara says. "Tell him what you told me."

Her father looks at me.

I suddenly wish I'd never brought it up.

I repeat word for word what I'd heard the preacher say at the Upper Room. I channel his intense energy, finishing with a final warning. "You have to burn it—you can't just throw it away."

With a cheeky look in his eye, her father laughs out loud.

I hold his gaze to let him know I'm serious, but I feel kind of foolish now.

Lara moves to stand directly in front of her father, pleading with him to listen.

He pulls her into a hug and laughs again. "I will not be *burning* any of my music today."

Fried-Bologna Sandwiches

Grandma is frying a big batch of bologna in a cast-iron pan. I stand beside her and take in the sizzle. It smells delicious. She fries until the pieces of bologna start to curl and the edges are slightly burnt. We're eating it for dinner tonight with white rice and a can of cream-style corn as a side.

Sometimes as a treat, Grandma will make fried bologna with macaroni and cheese for me and my cousins. It's our absolute favorite. We all sit at the table adding the finishing touch—ketchup, loads of it.

If there are leftovers, I will make a bologna sandwich as a snack. My mom won't let me take them to school for lunch, though. I am allowed to take the thinly sliced packaged bologna, not the thick ones we fry.

She makes up weird rules like that.

"Why can't I take *these* bologna sandwiches to school?" I ask.

"Only Indians and poor people eat this kind of bologna," she answers.

I think about her words as I make my sandwich. I turn the French's mustard container upside down and slowly squeeze it over a slice of white bread, forming a pattern with the mustard as I go. I place a piece of fried bologna on the bread, fold it in half and take a bite. It's that easy to make. The charred edges of the bologna mingle with mustard in my mouth. I suddenly forget that only poor people and us eat such things. I think they're delicious.

But after my mom forbids me to take them to school, I start checking out the other kids' school lunches. If you don't go home, or when it rains, you eat a bagged lunch brought from home in the gymnasium.

I study Native kids' sandwiches first. Most of them are the same as mine—one thin slice of bologna on white bread.

The white kids' sandwiches are fancy deli meat with lettuce and tomato, or egg salad, or peanut butter with banana. I've eaten deli meat at Lara's before. It's tasty.

One girl's sandwich is on brown bread and has weird-looking things coming out of it. She looks a bit sad.

"What is that?" I ask her.

Staring out from behind her glasses, she says, "Alfalfa sprouts."

It looks like moss to me. Maybe that's why she seems sad. I would be too if I had to eat that.

After school I tell my mom about the weird moss sandwich.

"Alfalfa sprouts," my mom says. "I think mostly hippies eat them."

I picture the moss in my mind and think about hippies. A few of them live on Digby Island. I wrinkle my nose and announce that I'd rather eat fried-bologna sandwiches over alfalfa sprouts any day.

Kids in Cars, Outside of Bars

It's late fall, and Uncle Jerry has a new burgundy-colored luxury van. It's so fancy. We're on our way to Hazelton for a weekend getaway. The adults announce that they need to stop for a "quick one" at a pub in Thornhill. I stay in the van with my cousins, Sherrie, Travis and Susan.

We never understand why the adults feel the need to go into a pub. As always, they have been sipping on beers since we left Rupert. And there's plenty more in the built-in cooler.

We're used to it, though. Besides, they always give us money to load up on more junk food. And they leave us the keys to turn the heat on if we need it.

We have been sitting in the van waiting for our parents for over an hour. I pop another strawberry-marshmallow candy into my mouth and stick my stained red tongue out at Susan.

"Stop eating them!" she laughs, as she puts another sunflower seed into her mouth.

Travis is sitting in the front passenger seat laughing his head off. He's reading a comic book. He's the middle child and mostly keeps to himself, reading and chewing on his fingernails.

Restlessness sets in. We take turns trying to call our parents out from the pub. "Susan, you go and call them," Sherrie says.

Susan is sitting in the driver's seat, looking at her reflection in the mirror. "You go. It's your turn, I went last time."

Sherrie tries another angle. "Mia, you go get them. They'll listen to you."

Why not. I'm bored anyway. I hunt around the van, looking for my shoes, put them on, climb out and make my way through the parking lot.

The pub's connected to a hotel, so to get there you have to go through the hotel lobby first. Then the pub entrance is down a hallway.

Of course, kids aren't allowed in bars, so I just stand in the doorway.

I spot my uncle right away—he's crouching over a pool table, his eyes focused on the cue ball, preparing to take a shot.

"Oh Sherrie" by Steve Perry is playing on a jukebox behind the pool table. It's a good song—Uncle Jerry owns the cassette.

The orange and purple patterns on the black carpet feel like a vast sea between my uncle and me, one I can't walk across.

He keeps making his shots, so it's still his turn. I watch him make his way around the pool table.

It's the middle of the day and the tables in the pub are mostly empty. My mom and aunt must be sitting around the corner, because I can't see them.

Uncle Jerry finally notices me and walks over.

He puts his arm around me and pulls me in tight for a hug. Pool cue still in hand, he says, "We'll go after this game, okay?"

I nod, hoping he means it.

The white man he's playing pool with misses his shot, so it's my uncle's turn again.

We say our goodbyes and I make my way out to the van.

After I deliver the update, Susan, still in the driver's seat, says, "We'll believe it when we see it."

Not long afterward, though, our parents walk back toward the van.

It's unspoken, but we're all experts in gauging the state of their soberness. We do it with a single glance.

This time they're fine.

Uncle Jerry isn't the biological father of my cousins. Their real dad died when they were very young. You'd never know, though. He loves them like they're his own.

He walks around to the side door of the van and calls Sherrie out.

Unsure of what's going on, she gets out of the van reluctantly.

Uncle Jerry gives her a twenty-dollar bill and a big warm hug.

He says he won it playing pool, and the reason he won was that the song "Oh Sherrie" was playing.

My cousin beams in her father's embrace.

Not just about the twenty dollars, which would make anyone happy, but because he'd made her feel special.

I'm just a kid and I can see that.

Traditional Foods

People within our community know we don't lock our front door. Sometimes we arrive home and there will be a sockeye or spring salmon in the kitchen sink. Or a bucket of clams on the counter.

Grandma's always surprised and happy. "I wonder who it's from," she says.

Grandma's considered an elder, so extended family and men from our reserve take good care of her. They provide her with seafood like halibut, herring eggs or dried seaweed. Always making sure she has plenty of good stuff on hand.

It's November and it's been pouring rain, windy and cold! We're used to it, though. It's close to dinnertime, so I make my way home from Lara's.

When I enter our house, a pungent aroma fills my nostrils. The smell isn't familiar to me.

The house is toasty warm, though, and a *Get Smart* rerun is on the television. It's one of Grandma and my favorite shows to watch together.

She's standing at the stove cooking and singing aloud. She does that often. She sings Christian songs, alternating between English and Sm'algyax.

I walk to the stove and stand beside her. She's stirring an unusually dark-colored stew. "What is that?" I ask, wrinkling my nose.

"Uula," she answers.

"*What?*" I ask.

"Seal meat," Grandma says, almost smiling into the pot. "Dem' guys just sent it in." She means sent it in from the reserve we belong to, which is Kitkatla.

"Eww, that is so gross!"

"Du wah, Amelia, be quiet," Grandma says. "You're not supposed to talk about our food like that."

"I *am not* eating that," I tell her.

She snaps her eyes at me, goes to the cupboard, grabs a quart jar of salmon and places it on the counter. I guess that's what I'll be eating for dinner instead of uula. What a funny word.

Disneyland and Messy Hair

For Christmas this year, my family and I went to Disneyland. My mom and I drove down with Uncle Jerry, Aunt Lorraine, their kids and my cousin Carmen. The ride was so long.

Uncle Ted, Aunt Becky, Tonya and David were there too. They arrived a few days before us. Our hotel was right across the street from Disneyland. And our rooms were all near each other—it was so much fun visiting back and forth!

We got a three-day pass for Disneyland, which gave us time to see everything. For Christmas Day, instead of eating turkey dinner, we ate spaghetti at a restaurant on Main Street in Disneyland.

It was also Grandma's birthday on Christmas Day. Earlier in the day we'd stumbled upon a huge phone booth. It looked like a normal booth except all twelve of us could fit inside, and there were even benches to sit on. We called Grandma collect and sang "Happy Birthday" to her on the speakerphone. It made me miss her and wish she was with us, but she couldn't have managed all this walking.

My cousins and I got autograph books to get signatures of all the characters. I liked Tigger the best. He was fun and teased me, poking the antenna balls on my headband. My mom got a picture of us.

When I asked Cinderella for her autograph, she leaned toward me, stared me in the eyes and said, "Can you say 'please'?"

I repeated my question and added "please."

But I wasn't as excited anymore. There were so many kids swarming her, and I did what everyone else did. She didn't ask any of them to say please.

Then my mom went and said, "Let me get your picture with Cinderella."

I barely smiled.

The lights were magical there. Like nothing I've ever seen. Twinkle lights of every kind lined the streets. My favorite ride by far was Peter Pan—it felt like we were actually flying! I'm thankful to Travis for insisting I go on. I wasn't planning to because I thought it was a boring boys' ride.

We all went on the Matterhorn too. I was scared, but Uncle Jerry said I could sit with him, and he assured me it would be fun. We sat in the front of the caboose, the rest of my cousins behind us. I leaned into Uncle Jerry, scared out of my wits, convinced I would fly out. It was all I could think about as the train slowly made its way to the top.

Once we reached the summit and started to descend, I closed my eyes tight and held on. During the first drop,

Uncle Jerry screeched in pure delight and yelled out, "Open your eyes!"

I did just as the caboose shot out of an opening. It felt like we were being ejected into the sky, until the tracks curved sharply, pulling us into a downward slope. I quickly closed my eyes again.

Behind me, I could hear my cousins happily shrieking the entire way.

I didn't open my eyes again until we reached the bottom.

We also went on the ride called It's a Small World, where they showcase different nations from around the world. At the very end of the water ride, in the last display, a couple of Native Indians appeared. Like an afterthought. At least, that's what I overheard my mom and Aunt Lorraine saying.

It definitely wasn't as elaborate as other nations' displays. But we managed to snap a quick picture of the Indian woman and little boy wearing deer hide.

We also spotted a wooden statue of an Indian Chief outside a storefront on Main Street and took pictures with it.

It had been a long day and everyone was tired, but we decided to stay longer because there was going to be a huge parade that night, followed by fireworks. We found a good spot to sit along the sidewalk on Main Street. We sat there for hours to save our seats.

My cousins and I had gotten the cutest matching Minnie Mouse sweatshirts. We were all wearing them, sitting in a row. Our moms took pictures of us.

The next day we went to Universal Studios to see where they make movies—it was amazing! We almost got attacked by Jaws and saw buildings on fire and a flooded street that practically reached our tour bus!

We also went to Knott's Berry Farm. I got a cartoon drawing of myself done. It looks exactly like me! Uncle Jerry got to be in it too because he was waiting for me while it was being drawn. The artist asked, "Is that your dad?" "He's my Uncle Jerry," I replied. So he drew him in. His baseball hat and all. He even wrote *Uncle Jerry* underneath.

We recognized some white people from Prince Rupert at the amusement park. We didn't know them, but we all waved and smiled from a distance.

We drove up the California Coast on our way back home. We stayed in San Francisco the first night. We rode the trolleys in the day, which was cool. There are so many steep hills there! They're practically as steep as the Matterhorn.

For dinner we ate on Fisherman's Wharf. I love clam chowder, so that's what I ordered and shared some of my mom's fish and chips.

She bought me a white hoodie that says *San Francisco* on the front. It has images of all the tourist spots on it. I didn't want it, because I know she's always worrying about money and how much things cost. I told her I already had my Minnie Mouse sweatshirt, but she insisted.

The only thing she's bought herself the whole trip is a Disneyland pen.

We got up early because we were going to drive over the Golden Gate Bridge. I am not a morning person. I had to drag myself out of bed before we headed to Denny's for breakfast.

The waitress sat us in a big round booth. It was only our main car group. We left Uncle Ted and them back in Anaheim (that's where Disneyland is).

Suddenly my mom said, "Mia, your hair is standing on end! Sheesh, brush it once in a while!" Everyone laughed. I held my menu higher so they couldn't see my hair, and they laughed even more. I wear my hair short and it's curly. I never bother with it much, as it seems to do its own thing anyway.

After three days of driving from Disneyland, we were finally back in Canada! We checked into the City Centre Motel in Vancouver.

Our parents were going to a New Year's Eve dance at the Indian Centre on East Hastings. Uncle Jerry went and picked up their tickets, and he bought us kids a bunch of fancy snacks since we'd be staying at the motel.

He got Ritz crackers, canned oysters, cheddar cheese, a coil of garlic sausage, mandarin oranges and a bottle that looks like champagne but really it's sparkling juice.

We had fun celebrating in the room and watched the ball drop on TV at midnight. I barely managed to stay awake for it, but I did.

We are on the final stretch now of our long trip. Uncle Jerry's from a different nation than us. He's Gitksan. We always stop and visit his family since we pass their reserve on the way.

I don't mind because I have a crush on a boy from his reserve.

We are getting closer, so I try to nap. But before I fall asleep I say to Susan, "Can you wake me up before we get there, so I can fix my hair?"

Everyone knows about my crush and they often tease me when they're drinking.

My mom says, "You walk all around California with messy hair and you finally think about fixing it when you're about to go onto a reserve!"

Everyone laughs.

All Native

The All Native Basketball Tournament is held every February in Prince Rupert. It started over twenty-five years ago and, as the name suggests, only Native people are allowed to play in it.

Hundreds of Natives flock into town from surrounding villages and faraway places like Alaska. I like seeing all the different people here.

The teams are usually named after the players' reserve or nation, followed by something like Sons, Braves or Warriors. Our team is the Kitkatla Warriors. But they usually get knocked out of the tournament right away.

My mom and I are going to watch the games tomorrow. Grandma doesn't watch basketball, probably because she's Christian.

When I was younger, I'd get bored of watching games so would go and play with kids under the bleachers. Now I sit and watch and cheer along with the crowd. Everyone hollers like crazy for their home team to win. It's a lot of fun.

We're sitting in the upper section waiting for the Trojans to play. They are the defending champions. They're a Prince Rupert team mixed with Natives who live in town but aren't playing for their own nation.

The team looks sharp coming out from the changeroom to warm up. Their uniforms this year have a logo of the Playboy bunny. I ask my mom to buy something with that logo on it. She says "No, that's not for kids."

My mom's cousin is playing on the team. He's tall and one of their star players. As soon as the game begins, they are ahead. Not long after, a woman sitting below us, who is cheering for the opposing team, starts going crazy. She yells out, "Why don't you go put a Playboy shirt on, ref!"

It's often the women who yell the most during the games. They say things like, "What, are you blind, ref?" "Foul!" Or "Defense!"

I start looking around and admiring the women's beautiful silver and gold West Coast carved Native jewelry. Some women wear bracelets practically up to their elbows. I always think that's what I want to look like when I grow up.

My mom is wearing her gold carved pendant and gold wolf earrings, which is our family's crest. I have a silver carved bracelet, but it's from when I was a baby so it doesn't fit me anymore.

Since the tournament is held annually, you start to recognize familiar faces. I see a girl I had played with under the bleachers the year before.

She smiles at me and we start talking to each other.

It doesn't take long for us to get friendly again. We go sit on the back staircase.

She's a very pretty girl. Her hair is curly and she wears it super short, even shorter than mine. She's wearing a bunch of silver carved bracelets on each wrist. It's rare to see kids with jewelry like that.

"I like your bracelets," I say.

"Thanks," she replies. She seems a bit shy.

She's wearing a red sweatershirt with a Native logo on it that says *Haida Gwaii Watchmen*.

"There you are!" a kid approaching us yells. "Your mom's looking for you."

"I have to go," the pretty girl says, smiling as she leaves.

I don't ask her name. I think I should have remembered it from the year before and am too embarrassed to ask.

The finals of the tournament come quickly. I never know the team we're rooting for half the time, but it's fun being in the stands.

On Saturday night, the adults go celebrate at bars or various dances around town. The dances are sponsored by different Native nations, like Nishga, Haida or Tsimshian—that's our nation.

Grandma absolutely insists I stay home on the weekend during the tournament. She says it's too wild in town.

After one week of our little town buzzing with excitement, the Civic Centre parking lot packed, and No Vacancy signs at every hotel, it is all over. Until next year.

White Friends

Abby is a classmate whose family attends the Native Pentecostal. She has brown skin and a solid build. She wears her thick black hair in two short braids with colorful bobbly elastics.

We are on recess break and I see her talking to a group of Native girls.

I'm walking alone, so I slow my steps and inch my way toward them.

Abby stops talking and looks at me. Her face says, *Can I help you with something?* even though she doesn't speak.

I smile sweetly at her.

"What, no white friends for you to hang around with today?" she asks. Her tone is razor-sharp.

I can't believe she said that!

I've never had problems with her before. We've played together at church many times.

I don't reply. I just adjust my direction and walk past them.

Her words repeat over and over in my mind. *What, no white friends for you to hang around with today?*

Lara isn't Native and she is my best friend. Is that what Abby means?

I start going down the list of my other school friends— they aren't Native either. I guess I haven't thought about things in that way before. Or maybe I have?

College Roommates

It's a Monday morning, and Lara and I are walking to school. We are almost done fifth grade. She brings up something we've never discussed before.

"When we go to college, we'll be roommates."

We? College? She sounds so certain, I believe her.

My fate has been decided. I am going to college, even though just a few minutes earlier the idea had never entered my mind.

Lara tells me her dad is already saving for her college fund.

Fund?

My mind begins racing.

I'm no longer following the conversation.

Firstly, my grades are dreadful. I know there is no way I would get into college. And even if I manage to pick up my grades, which I've done in the past, my mom doesn't have money for that kind of thing.

We often have to dig through pockets looking for spare money to take a cab to the laundromat downtown.

Lara is still talking. Thankfully, she hasn't noticed I spaced out.

"I want to be an ophthalmologist," she says.

A what?

Was that a joke? Do I laugh? Or should I look sad? The word she said certainly sounded sad.

By the time we reach school, my mind is reeling. I can't even pronounce what my best friend said she wants to be when she grows up, let alone explain what it is. The conversation is too much for my ten-year-old brain.

I reflect on our discussion over the next few days. I think of various ways I could get money to go to college so Lara and I could be roommates, just like she'd said.

I mention the idea of college to my mom during the commercial break of *Night Court,* her favorite show.

"I took nursing at Vancouver Community College," she replies. "But then I got pregnant with you."

My mom is a woman of few words. She mostly speaks at you rather than to you. When she does speak, though, it's usually something memorable that sticks.

Like the time she told me my nostrils were so big you could drive a semi-truck up them. I went and got a mirror and held it under my nose, stretching my nostrils as far as they could go.

Or when she found out I had a crush on a Native boy from another reserve. My mom said he wasn't *good enough* for me. I kind of understood what she meant.

Later that day, I found myself sitting on the edge of my bed, ignoring the throb of my tender heart, and began slowly cutting up the wallet-sized school picture he'd given me.

I watched as one eye, his nose, then his smile fell to my lap like a jigsaw puzzle.

A few days after the college conversation, if you can call it that, my mom and I are washing clothes at the laundromat. We decide to walk and get a pizza while our clothes are in the dryer.

Most of the stores are closed Sundays, so the streets are quiet. We're making our way toward the pizza place at the end of the block when a window sign catches my eye—*Ophthalmologist.*

There it is.

I sound it out under my breath.

The shop is closed so I go to the window to look inside. It's an eye doctor's clinic. So that's what it is.

My mom looks confused. She knows my eyes are fine, excellent even. "Mia, what are you doing?" she asks.

I keep looking through the glass. "This is what Lara wants to be when she grows up," I say.

Ophthalmologist. I say the word again.

"You have to be really smart to do that," my mom says.

That's her reply about a lot of things.

"Lara *is* smart," I say as I step back from the window. "She gets mostly A's."

The next time I see Lara I bring up college and her being an ophthalmologist.

I act all casual as I say it, but inside I'm pleased I'd pronounced it correctly and that I know what it is.

Lara mumbles something about not wanting to be an ophthalmologist anymore and changes the subject.

Salmonberry Picking

June is salmonberry season. They come just before the salmon season. That's how we know the fish will be arriving.

Aunt Carol, her husband John, their son Michael, Grandma, my mom and I are going berry picking this afternoon. Grandma brought every empty bucket she could find from home.

We find a spot off the side of the highway, just outside of town. The bushes are loaded. It's the first time Grandma's been picking with us in a long time. I stay close by in case she needs help. I worry she'll trip over a stump or something.

Grandma doesn't seem concerned at all. She's not moving her legs much, mostly using her arms and reaching like a pro. She pulls down branches to get to the ones behind or higher up.

I hear my mom speak quietly through shrubs. "Mia, are you keeping an eye on your grandma?"

"Yeah," I answer.

The berries are big and juicy.

I sample a few.

If anyone sees you eating too many, they'll say, "Hey now," half kidding, half not. Berry picking is serious business.

There are dark purple ones, bright red ones and orange ones that are the same color as orange popsicles.

I pick a purple berry, examine it for any bugs, then pop it into my mouth.

A few years ago, Grandma sent six of us kids berry picking. She tied string around the side handles of ice-cream pails and placed them around our necks.

"Huh?" I said.

Grandma motioned, making like she was picking berries, using both hands and dropping them in an imaginary bucket in front of her.

"Oh," I said, nodding my head. I got it. My cousins did too.

We headed to Seal Cove, a neighborhood known for having a lot of salmonberries. We hit the bushes like a pack of wolves.

It wasn't until we were in action ourselves that we saw the genius of Grandma's buckets. Both hands were busy, pulling at branches and picking every berry in sight.

We also found blueberries and filled one whole bucket. Mary, who was the oldest among us, was quite pleased with that and said, "Big Mom will love these."

In no time, our buckets were filled.

We were making our way back home when Mary spotted a huge boulder with bushes on top.

"Look," she said, pointing to the boulder. "Those are blueberry bushes up there."

She spotted a path that led to the top. "Come on, guys, let's go look."

"Nah. I don't want to," I said. "It's too high and I'm getting tired."

"Quit being lazy, Mia!"

"You guys go. I can stay down here with all the berries."

"Hey, that's a good idea. We won't have to lug them up," Mary said.

We combined the berries to empty a bucket that they could use to pick the blueberries. "Okay, come on, kids," Mary said, motioning with her hands.

My cousins followed and made their way up the rock like brown-skinned explorers in search of gold.

Partway up the climb, Mary turned around and hollered, "And don't eat any of the berries, Mia!"

"I won't," I mumbled. I was tired and already dreading the walk back home.

I found a stump to sit on and wait. I was surrounded by buckets and buckets of colorful berries.

Up the hill, I could hear them oohing and aahing at all the blueberries they found. Mary was an excellent berry picker, really fast.

I decided to sample a blueberry from Mary's bucket while I waited.

They were so tasty and refreshing. I grabbed another handful.

"Whoa, over here!" I heard Mary call. I continued eating.

When they came back down, the first words out of Mary's mouth were "Mia!! You ate almost all the blueberries!"

"They dumped." The lie came out of nowhere.

Mary's eyes darted to the ground around me. "There's no blueberries on the ground! And your mouth is all blue!"

I just sat there.

"How could you do that? You are just rotten, Mia," she added.

"I was hungry," I responded sheepishly.

"And I'm telling Big Mom what you did." Then she added, "At least we got another bucket up there. But you're still going to be in trouble."

She was right. I could already hear Grandma saying, *You're a bad girl, Amelia.*

Mary fussed with the buckets, handing one to each of us to carry back.

"*I'll* hold on to *these*," she said, cradling the freshly picked bucket of blueberries as she looked over her shoulder at me.

When we walked in the door, Grandma's eyes lit up at the sight of our filled buckets. We covered the kitchen counter with an array of colorful berries.

"Oh my!" Grandma said as she grabbed a large enamel bowl to start washing them.

My cousins crowded behind her, saying, "And Mia ate most of the blueberries!" They all spoke at once, pointing their fingers at me, like Grandma didn't know who Mia was.

"Look, her mouth is still blue," my cousin Carmen threw in. She loves to tattle on me like that.

Grandma was too delighted with all the berries to pay any attention, only glanced over her shoulder at me.

I went and grabbed plastic freezer bags from the drawer and placed them on the counter next to her.

She didn't say anything, just continued rinsing the berries. After that, she divided them into bags to freeze for the winter.

We ate some of them later, mixed with oolichan grease and sugar. It's one of my favorite desserts.

Crooked Teeth and Mountain Bikes

This summer Lara and Owen got new bikes to replace the ones that had been stolen. It was bye-bye banana-seat bike and hello Norco-brand mountain bike.

Lara said their insurance covered the expense. The new bikes seemed so grown-up. They were modern and beyond anything the rest of us Pigott Avenue kids could afford.

I was happy for them, but I missed her banana-seat bike. We couldn't double anymore, and since they weren't allowed to lend their new bikes to anyone, I mostly watched them ride.

I'd outgrown my BMX bike, which I never really liked anyway. And I hadn't gotten a new bike since that one. I didn't tell my mom about Lara's new bike. But she must have seen it in my sullen face.

Not long afterward she bought me a brand-new Norco mountain bike too.

However, it wasn't like on *The Price Is Right* when a screen door opens and the announcer yells, "A new bike!" and the contestant jumps up and down screaming.

Yes, I got a new bike and it's really cool, but I knew we couldn't afford it. The bike came at a cost.

The dentist had recently informed us that I needed braces (they are so expensive!). The Department of Indian Affairs only approved paying for half. My mom has been working long hours at the cannery this summer, often doing twelve-hour shifts, and she saved the money for the rest of the braces.

One day she presented me with an interesting offer.

She said I could get a mountain bike or braces.

That probably sounds like the most ridiculous thing you've ever heard.

And you're right. It kind of is.

My mom's a single parent and a seasonal worker. She couldn't afford braces *and* a mountain bike.

She said my teeth weren't *that bad*. I also know she likes to provide me with nice things. I barely understand how adult stuff works, but I could tell it was hard for her to tell me I had to pick.

I chose the bike.

There were so many colors to choose from. I decided on a lime-green model with white accents.

It's so nice! I feel good riding down the street. As I ride through different neighborhoods, friends from school say,

"Whoa, nice bike, Mia!" And I no longer have to sit and watch Lara ride. Now we are the same when we go biking.

It's Wednesday evening. My mom and I decide to go visit my cousin Patti. She takes a cab and I ride my bike. By the time I arrive, they're already having a beer.

I go say hello and talk to them for a few minutes and then go back outside to ride my bike. I act like it's a motorcycle. I practice my parking, reversing into spots, never pulling directly in.

I go into the house to ask my mom something, leaving my bike parked in the driveway. My mom and Patti seem to be enjoying their beers, getting "tipsy," as they say.

When I come back out my bike is gone.

I run to the sidewalk, look left and then right. Nothing. I stand there stunned.

I run back inside, devastated. When I tell my mom about my bike, she seems at a loss for words, then glares at me. "Nothing you can do about it now," she says, and then reaches for her beer.

Patti looks genuinely upset for me. "Well, that sucks, Mia. I'm sorry," she says.

They go back to their conversation. I just stand there. Still stunned.

No one offers to look into other people's yards to try to find my bike.

I go into the bathroom, slide down the wall to the floor and cry my eyes out.

It *Was* the Indians!

The following week my mom and I go over to Aunt Lorraine's for a visit. My mood is still low over my stolen bike.

Aunt Lorraine lives a few houses down from Patti's. We walk into their kitchen and I can't believe my eyes—leaning against a wall in the back room off the kitchen is my bike!

"Mia's bike!" my mom says, equally surprised.

"Travis," my aunt says, shrugging her shoulders.

My cousin Travis had stolen it. In this case, it *was* the Indians.

And how fortunate for me that the person who stole it just so happens to be my cousin.

I make my way toward the bike in disbelief, as if it's an optical illusion and if I reach out for it, it will disappear.

I place my hands on the handles, and a sense of relief floods through me. I turn the bike around, steering, braking, navigating my way through the house, and bring it outside.

I ride and ride and ride my bike. Up and down hills, over bumpy gravel, zigzagging down the middle of the street and, of course, working on my reverse parking.

My cousin Travis said he knew that it was my bike outside of Patti's. He said that he was teaching me a lesson and that I shouldn't have been so stupid as to leave an expensive bike unlocked like that.

I thought it was mean, but I've learned my lesson, all right.

Cute Native Boy

It's the end of summer, and my cousin Mel is visiting from Kitkatla. We're close, so I'm excited she's in town.

We are making our way back to the laundromat where we're supposed to be helping Grandma. Instead, we go to the corner store to get junk food, and linger longer than we should have. Suddenly, I catch sight of a cute Native boy walking toward us.

He's fairer-skinned and is wearing dark blue jeans and a button-up shirt. He looks like he's around the same age as me but seems older. And confident.

He nods as he walks past us.

"Who is that?" I whisper.

"Oh, that's Jeff Roberts. He's from Kitkatla," Mel says.

"He's so cute!" I say, glancing over my shoulder.

"His mom was a teacher out there," Mel adds.

"How come I've never seen him there before?" I ask.

Mel shrugs her shoulders, as if it's every day there's a cute boy from Kitkatla.

It turns out his grandparents own a general store in Kitkatla. I'm aware of who they are, and I've shopped at their store many times, but I've never seen him.

"He lives in town now, though," Mel adds.

"*What?* Are you kidding?"

"You're crazy," Mel says. Like she's done with boy talk for the day.

The following week Lara and I are sitting in her rec room, and she tells me she has a crush on a boy who lives across town. She says he has blond hair and blue eyes. Lara mostly has crushes on Native boys. We don't talk about them being Native—it's just an observation I've made.

I don't change crushes as frequently as she does, so I'm glad to have something to contribute to the conversation. I tell her about the cute boy I saw with Mel. "And get this, he's from Kitkatla!" I say.

"What?" Lara's mouth drops.

She doesn't know anything about our reserve other than it's where I disappear to now and again. I say "disappear" because my family doesn't always plan ahead for things. When my mom or Grandma says we're going to Kitkatla, we just up and go.

Sometimes I don't even get a chance to let Lara know I'll be away, which, of course, upsets her. One time I was gone for four months. Lara cried and told her mom I was never coming back.

She's excited to hear about my new crush and wants all the details.

But there aren't any. I walked past him. The end.

I don't know where the idea came from or who decided it was a good one. We have certainly never prank-called boys before, yet suddenly we find ourselves reaching for the phone book, looking up phone numbers like a couple of pros.

Lara goes first. She dials up her new crush.

"Hi, Chad! How's it going?" She holds the phone so we can both hear.

"It's going," he says. "Who is this?"

"What are you up to?" she asks, ignoring his question.

"Eating a popsicle," he answers.

She laughs, like he's spoken the most adorable words ever. "What color?" she asks while fanning her face with her hand.

"Purple," he replies, then adds, "Seriously, who is this?"

"Well, gotta run, *bye!*" Lara hangs up the phone and we both roll on the carpet in nervous laughter.

We go over every detail of the conversation.

"Eating a purple popsicle…" Lara says dreamily. Then she snaps out of it and says, "Okay, it's your turn."

We consult the phone book once again. There's only one Roberts in the phone book. Could it be the cute Native boy's phone number? I dial nervously and wait while it rings.

A woman picks up. "Is Jeff there, please?" I'd learned from my white friends that you should say "please" when asking for things.

"Hold on a moment," the lady responds.

I chicken out at the last minute and hand the phone to Lara. I move in close again so I can hear.

"Hello," we hear a deep voice say.

Lara covers the receiver with her hand and screeches, "Mia, he sounds like a man!"

"Hello?" the deep voice says again.

I reach for the base of the phone and push the thingy down to hang up.

We break into laughter once again.

"How old did you say he was?!" Lara asks.

"Twelve."

We break out laughing again.

"We have to call back!" she says.

"No way!" I snicker.

We call it a day on prank calls.

Permed-Hair Disaster

Lara is pretty. She has a beauty mark right above her lip, just like Madonna's! She owns all of Madonna's cassettes; we're totally obsessed with her music. We spend endless hours in Lara's bedroom talking about school and boys and Madonna's incredible sense of style. How if we were older and lived somewhere like Vancouver, we'd totally dress like her.

Lara has already begun incorporating bits and pieces of "Madonna-like" fashion into her wardrobe, like lace headbands and stuff. And I can always tell if she's had a disagreement with her mother because she wears loud mismatched earrings as a way of rebelling.

We've just started sixth grade. Thankfully, Lara and I are in the same class once again.

I let my mom know I need money for school photos. We always order the largest package because we have such a big family. I have twenty-one first cousins.

Like I said before, I have always had short unruly hair. My mom was never the "sit down and let me braid your hair" kind of mom, so I'm guessing she kept it short so she wouldn't have to deal with it. And it's never occurred to me to grow it out.

"Why don't you try perming your hair for picture day?" my mom asks.

She and her sisters all wear their hair the same—short and permed.

I don't put too much effort into the way I look. "Sure," I say, shrugging my shoulders.

"I'll book you an appointment with Corrine," my mom says.

Corrine is her hairstylist. She's Asian, affordable and can fit me in right away.

Sitting in the salon, I tell Corrine I'd like her to use big rods for loose curls, more of a spiral perm. It seems to be the latest fashion craze.

She says my hair is too short for that.

"Okay, whatever you think."

The black plastic cape drapes me like a tent. I watch in the mirror as she wraps strands of hair around row after row of rods. It's my first perm. I'm surprised at how long the process takes. The solution is *so* strong and smelly.

I shift restlessly in my seat.

I've seen my mom and grandma get perms many times, but I smile at my reflection when she's finished with the rods. I look like I'm from Mars or something.

After she's done rinsing the solution out and I'm sitting back in the chair, she removes the towel from my head. My hair is curly, all right!

I'm excited to see what she'll do with it. She begins blow-drying my hair on a low setting, then snips at pieces of hair here and there with scissors.

A look of satisfaction spreads across her face as she smooths a wisp along my hairline with her finger.

I start to worry. It doesn't look done to me.

"How do you like it?" she asks.

I stare at my reflection in the mirror.

I look like my mom and aunties. I'd fit right in at bingo.

I force a smile and surprise myself by saying, "I like it, thank you."

After we pay and leave the salon, my mom says, "It looks nice, Mia."

Nice? I give her a stone-cold glare. Who wants to look nice?

"I want to go home!" I say sharply. I wouldn't be caught dead in public with this hair.

As we taxi home, I remember the stylist's strict instructions. *Don't wash your hair for a few days, or it will wash the perm out.*

We walk in the door and I wave hello at Grandma sitting in her corner chair.

Her eyes zero in on my curls. Even Grandma knows I look ridiculous.

I go straight to the bathroom, grab the hose, lean my head over the tub and soak my head. I fill the palm of my hand with shampoo until it's almost overflowing, rub it onto my hair, then rinse and repeat with conditioner.

My mom's standing in the doorway. "You're not supposed to wash it! You'll ruin it."

"That's the point!" I yell out angrily.

"You're wasting my money!"

I let the sound of the water drown her out.

Picture day is next Thursday. What am I going to do? I turn the water off, wrap a towel around my head, walk to my room and close the door. I have my own room right now because there are no other family members living with us.

When I remove the towel, the curls are still there. I put a glob of gel in my hand and run my fingers through my hair and let it air-dry.

I decide to lie down, read a Sweet Valley High book and *not* think about my perm.

An hour later I go look in the mirror. I'm a dead ringer for Michael Jackson on the cover of his *Thriller* album. Don't get me wrong. I love Michael Jackson. When he burned his hair a few years ago filming a commercial, my cousin Michael called me immediately to see if I was watching the news.

I pick up the telephone and call Lara to tell her I got a perm.

She shrieks so loudly I have to move the receiver away from my ear. "Mia, you have to come over!"

"I'm on my way."

Before leaving, I glance in the mirror and push down on the curls to flatten them, but it's no use.

I ring her doorbell. I gently kick at an overhanging brick on a planter. I should have worn a hat. That would flatten the curls, or at least hide them.

Lara opens the door and her mouth drops open.

I stand awkwardly, not knowing what to say.

It crosses my mind that maybe she likes it. Is that why she's speechless?

I force a smile and motion with my hands like *ta-da*.

She bursts out laughing and can't stop.

"Don't laugh at me!"

"Okay, I'm sorry." She stops, but then starts laughing again, harder this time. She even leans forward and slaps her knee.

I turn around to walk back home.

"Mia, I'm sorry!" Lara manages to compose herself. "Come in."

She's staring straight ahead to keep from laughing, trying so hard that her eyes are going crossed.

We go to her room and stand in front of her dresser mirror.

She seems to be done laughing. She moves so she's facing me. Staring, deep in thought like an artist examining a sculpture.

Then, as if she's had a creative breakthrough, she reaches for her dresser handle and pulls out a lace ribbon.

She puts her hand on my chin and gently turns my face toward her, places the ribbon at the base of my neck, ties it into a bow on top of my head and then adjusts it so it sits slightly to the right.

Her eyes light up. "There."

I look in the mirror. My long neck is still topped with a head of curls, but they're now contained, shaped by a single strand of lace.

"You fixed it!" A glimmer returns to my eyes, color to my face, and I smile slightly at the reflection.

"It's really cute," Lara says.

I nod my head quickly in agreement. It *is* cute. A look I've never gone for, but it will have to do.

When we receive our school pictures, I am pleased with the results. It's one of my better school photos.

Dance Lessons

Lara's been in jazz dance lessons for years. She's taught me some moves, like how to place my arms in a dance brace. Shoulders back, chin up, and then chassé. She often makes up dance routines for us, which she calls choreography.

I beg my mom to let me join jazz as well, and I'm thankful when she eventually enrols me.

I know we don't have a lot of extra money, so I'm always appreciative when she lets me join extracurricular activities like swimming, soccer, gymnastics and now jazz dance!

We don't own a vehicle, so getting to classes or practice is challenging.

When soccer is in season, practice is held at a school field at the opposite end of town. Uncle Jerry drives me once in a while, but if his hockey team is on television, he doesn't.

Swimming is right after school, so it's easy to walk or take a bus to and from if I have change for fare.

. Dance classes are held in the fall through spring, and they start at 7:00 p.m. I can take the last bus there at 6:30 p.m. but unfortunately have no way of getting home afterward.

The other girls' parents drop them off and pick them up when class is over.

I'm too embarrassed to let anyone know we don't own a car, so I try to slip out unnoticed. If anyone questions how I'm getting home, I usually say, "I'm going to my aunt's place, just right over there."

A half-hour walk home after dark when you're eleven years old isn't ideal, but there's nothing I can do.

The dance gear for class is expensive as well. My mom bought me black leather dance shoes that cost over fifty dollars—they were the cheapest ones we could find. The leggings were also costly, but we found a pair on sale. They are a sheen opal color. I feel like a brown-skinned Jamie Lee Curtis in them.

We didn't have enough money for a bodysuit. I didn't want my mom to feel bad, so I told her it would be no problem to use my bathing suit over top.

I have dance class tonight and of course I'm running late and end up missing the last bus.

I start to walk to class as I've done many times before. It wouldn't be so bad if it weren't pouring rain out. And to make matters worse, I couldn't find an umbrella. Not that anyone in Prince Rupert ever uses umbrellas. It's too windy for them.

I arrive late looking like a drowned rat. A sopping-wet mess.

I go to the washroom and use paper towels to try and dry off. I wore my tights under my blue jeans, and as I start to undress I realize the blue dye ran all over my new tights. They are no longer opal—they are now sky blue.

Now they *really* don't match my bathing suit colors of black, fuchsia and yellow.

I dab at my wet hair with paper towel but it's no use. I stare at my reflection in the mirror and let out a heavy sigh.

Class has already started. The girls are standing against the mirror-lined wall, wearing their stylish (and matching) dance gear.

The instructor has them doing exercises one by one. "Step, ball, change," she says, over and over.

I tiptoe across the old wooden dance floor, hoping no one will notice that I'm late, I'm soaking wet and my previously improvised dance gear is now even more mismatched.

I reach the railing and lean one arm against it. The soft wood brings some comfort.

A girl beside me whispers, "Did you walk here in the rain or something?"

I quietly chuckle. "Yeah. My mom couldn't drive me today."

I couldn't believe I outright lied like that.

I Have a Plan

Lara is clever at outsmarting anyone who causes trouble for us.

A tough girl named Tracy, who is a year older than us, came to our sixth-grade class. It was just before the afternoon lesson began, so we were already sitting at our desks.

In a threatening tone, Tracy says, "I'll see you two after school."

Lara and I look at each other.

What does that mean? Is she going to try and fight us?

We pass notes back and forth in the afternoon discussing the possible meaning of her words.

Do you know what this is about? Lara's note says.

No idea, I scribble back.

When the after-school bell rings, Lara marches to my desk with an assured look in her eyes. "I have a plan," she says.

I stare, waiting to hear it.

She continues, "Let's go to her class right now and show her we're not afraid."

We quickly grab our jackets from the cloakroom. I feel adrenaline pumping through my veins. The seventh-grade classroom is right next to ours. Tracy is still sitting at her desk even though most of the kids have left.

We stand in the doorway, waiting.

After a while Lara, in a calm, matter-of-fact voice, says, "Tracy, we're here. What did you want to see us about?"

Tracy's face turns as red as her hair. Clearly, she didn't believe we would show up.

"How long will you be?" Lara asks.

"I have to stay late," Tracy mumbles angrily and turns away.

"Okay. Well, we have to go," Lara says and turns to leave.

I don't know what else to do, so I give her a quick wave and say, "See you, Tracy."

Lara and I giggle as we make our way home in the crisp winter afternoon. We are quite pleased with ourselves for pulling one over on the school bully.

"We sure showed her!" Lara says, boxing into the air with her mittens.

Lara always comes up with original ideas like that. One time in fifth grade, I was whispering with a classmate when I should have been listening to the teacher.

The teacher called on me to answer a question, even though my hand wasn't up. I hadn't heard the question, so how could I answer?

My classmates started turning to look at me, waiting for a reply.

Lara's desk was in the same row as mine but at the front. Even she turned around. *Go ahead, Mia, answer the teacher*, was what her look was saying.

The teacher allowed the silence to linger a bit longer to make her point. Then she called on someone else, who promptly provided the correct answer.

A few weeks later, the teacher called on Lara with a question when she was in the middle of a conversation with a classmate. She hadn't been listening either. She looked down at her textbook, then at the chalkboard, as if trying to quickly figure out the answer.

Then she boldly replied, "I don't know the answer."

The teacher hesitated for a moment and then moved on to another student.

After that it became *a thing*.

Anytime anyone is called on unprepared, "I don't know the answer" is the reply.

Go Back to *Town*

The incident with Tracy reminds me of when I was in second grade and my mom and I unexpectedly up and moved to Kitkatla. The furnace had conked out at our house, and we didn't have money to buy a new one. It was going to be a long, cold winter, so my mom decided we needed a more liveable place to stay.

I enrolled in school *out* there. That's the way people talk there—they say, *out* Kitkatla or *out* home. And they call Prince Rupert *in* town.

We had moved in with my mom's younger sister, her husband and their three kids. This is my cousin Mel's family. She's a year younger than me.

Girls my age joined Beaver Scouts, and I was fortunate to have moved there the first week the program started, so I joined as well.

I was already familiar with the routine of extra-curricular activities from living in town. We were all given white T-shirts that had *Beaver* written across the chest in red letters. We were assigned our first lesson, to memorize the Beaver's honor code for the next week. It was one paragraph long. If we memorized it word for word, we'd get our first badge.

I practiced and practiced with my mom. The following week after the bell rang, us girls ran the short distance from school to our Beaver meeting, which was held in an adjacent building. As soon as we got there, our group leader, who was the village priest's non-Native wife, asked, "Who's memorized the assignment?"

I was the only one to raise my hand.

"Mia, stand up," she said.

I stood and recited the entire paragraph, just as we were instructed to do.

The leader seemed impressed and arched a thin, almost translucent eyebrow to show it.

I was then presented with my first badge.

Mel and I usually bathed together before bed. If I went to sleep with wet hair, as I often did, it was a wild mess in the morning.

The mirror above the bathroom sink was too high for me to see my reflection, so I didn't usually pay much attention to how I looked. Once in a while, I would stand on the toilet and lean over for a quick peek. Like the time Mel and I went to a boy's birthday party. Otherwise, no one at school seemed to care about that kind of stuff.

The day after I received my badge at the Beaver meeting, I stopped to pick up my new friend Rachel on the way to school.

Her older brother answered the door as usual and said Rachel had left for school already. I continued making my way, arriving just in time for the bell.

We had our Sm'algyax language class that morning. An elderly lady from the village, Mrs. Roy, came in to teach us. Our regular teacher was white.

Mrs. Roy taught us how to name our facial features like eyes, ears, nose and mouth in Sm'algyax by getting us to stand and sing a song.

At the end she'd say, "Wayi wansm," which I quickly learned meant "everyone, sit down."

After that, I'd try to be the fastest one to sit, so Mrs. Roy knew I understood what she meant.

I'd felt proud that I was catching on so quickly. At home I'd show off to my family and say "wayi wansm" before we ate dinner.

Then we had a spelling test. I liked spelling because it was so easy.

At recess, I walked outside looking for my friend. When I spotted Rachel, I headed toward her. She was standing with a bunch of girls from class. They were all leaning against a metal railing. Rachel was kind of pretty and fair-skinned. Something seemed off with her that morning. I started to slow down, unsure about walking any closer.

Rachel yelled out to me, "When you call at my house, my brother says, 'The girl with the messy hair is here,'" and started to laugh.

It was a gloriously wicked laugh. The other girls joined in.

I stood opposite them, with my unruly head of messy hair, feeling like the last one to be picked in a game of Red Rover.

This meanness seemed to have come out of nowhere. The day before, they were my sweet classmates. Now these girls were more like a pack of wolves. Eyeing me like I was easy prey.

I was skilled at concealing my emotions. I turned on my heels and walked in the opposite direction.

They cackled even more.

After school I told my mom what happened. My mom figured it was about the badge I'd received at the Scout meeting the day before. "They're jealous because they didn't get a badge."

At the next Scout meeting, I walked in wearing my T-shirt with my badge sewn on. I could see the other girls staring at it, but everyone was on their best behavior.

This time around, almost every one of them had memorized the honor code and got their badges.

Even the ones who hadn't memorized it got a badge.

After that, I assumed everything would go back to normal because we were all the same—we all had badges.

But it did not.

Rachel and I made up, sort of, but what she'd started with the other girls stuck. What's worse, their older sisters were now picking on me too.

I was suddenly considered a village outsider. When I passed the girls they'd say things to me like, "Why don't you go back to *town!*"

It was mostly one family of sisters. It was never just one of them either—they were always together. And these girls were built solid, solid like trunks of trees.

I was a slim build. Like a twig in comparison, a twig they wanted to snap.

But I was a fast runner. Those tree stumps couldn't catch me if they tried.

I was walking alone one day, and when I came around the corner by the nursery school, there they were.

I hesitated but didn't want them to think I was afraid to walk past, so I took my chances and kept on.

Sure enough, they jumped off the monkey bars and started after me.

I picked up my pace, but they followed.

They were getting close, so I ducked into the Church Army building. I went directly to the basement, thinking I could wait things out.

Then I heard the creak of the door.

They'd followed me into a church? *What was wrong with these people?*

The vibrations from their feet rushing down the stairs sent tingles up my spine. I was trapped.

I suddenly remembered there was a back door. I had seconds to escape, so I ran for it.

As I exited through the back I heard Dawn, who was in seventh grade, say, "Someone go out the front door and we'll trap her!" She was the alpha of the pack.

My mom had an uncle who lived across the street from the church. He and his wife, May, were older, churchgoing folks who often traveled to various communities preaching the message. My grandmother and I had joined them on those trips.

I made a dash for their doorstep with the girls hot on my heels.

Out of breath, my heart pounding, I knocked on their door and, without waiting for them to answer, entered their home.

I did my best to act casual, like I was dropping by to visit. "Hi, Ya'as," I said. It means "grandfather." "How are you guys?"

There was an old wooden chair that sat at the front door. I collapsed into it, exhausted.

If Ya'as replied to my question, I didn't hear him, as my thoughts were on the pack of wolves outside the door, waiting to tear at my flesh with their claws. At least, that's what I imagined they'd do if they ever caught me.

I peeked outside through the sheer curtains—they were still out there.

My visit wasn't fooling anyone. Great-Aunt May never said anything at the time, but she saw it all.

A few weeks later Mel and I were walking around close to dinnertime, and the girls were in the same spot. It must have been their hangout.

The moment they saw us they jumped off the monkey bars and walked toward us.

I nudged Mel. "Come on, let's go," I said as I turned in the opposite direction.

Dawn's best friend, whose name was Tina, was suddenly standing in front of me, blocking me from walking any farther.

"I need the washroom," I blurted out. I'm not sure why. I tried moving around her.

Tina was a basketball player with an athletic build. She blocked me as if on the court. "Go right there," she said, motioning to a big puddle.

Everyone laughed, including Mel, but hers was a high-pitched, overly nervous laugh.

Tina didn't take her eyes off me. I'd never even talked to her before! But she was out for blood. She had me trapped.

I made a split-second-decision move. I bolted to her left and ran for it.

I felt sick about leaving Mel behind, but I didn't dare look back.

I ran home without stopping. When I burst through the door, I shouted, "They've got Mel!"

Uncle Bo looked up from his chair and quickly went to throw on his shoes, asking, "Where are they?" as he tied his laces.

"At the nursery school by the monkey bars," I replied, out of breath.

He grabbed his hoodie from the wall hook and was off.

Not long afterward, Uncle Bo and Mel walked through the door calm as can be, like they were returning from an afternoon stroll.

I breathed a sigh of relief.

Mel said they didn't say or do anything to her. Then she laughed and said, "You looked so funny running that fast!"

Everyone settled into the living room to watch television.

I pretended like I wasn't upset. I tried to ignore my heart that was still pounding, my mind still racing. *Why do these girls dislike me so much?*

I was tall for my age—maybe they thought I was older.

Mel was younger and short. And she lived in Kitkatla. She was one of them.

It was me they didn't like. Me they wanted to *go back to town*.

When a commercial came on, Aunty Jean leaned over and said, "Those girls' mothers used to chase after me and try to beat me up when I was your age."

I nodded my head.

It was all I needed to hear.

That Friday, on lunch break at school, I was playing off the school grounds but in a safe spot in front of a store. It wasn't really a store—it was someone selling homemade goodies like bread, pies and popcorn balls from their home.

Suddenly my mom showed up, carrying a couple of bags, and said, "Come on, we're going into town."

I was surprised but happy to go along, as we'd gone into town for weekends before. We flew to Rupert by seaplane.

After enjoying the weekend in town, the following Monday morning my mom informed me we would not be returning to Kitkatla. At first I objected.

My mom said that Aunt May had gone on the CB radio a while back and told my mom in Sm'algyax about me running into their house because girls were trying to beat me up.

She'd ignored it, thinking Aunt May was being overly protective. But after what happened to Mel and me, my mom said, "No way, we're outta here."

"But they never caught me! I'm a fast runner!" I said.

"I don't care," she responded.

I was sad at the news. I'd grown to love living on the reserve. I loved everything about it, school, our Sm'algyax language class, playing down by the beach, the smell of woodstoves and, of course, all the delicious seafood.

I made one last attempt. "Mom, I'm fine," I said, almost begging. "I can take care of myself. Can we go back now, please?"

"Drop it," my mom said. "We aren't going back."

Secret Admirer

It's spring of sixth grade. I still have a crush on Todd Anderson from back in fifth grade. He's the boy whose desk was near the pencil sharpener and the reason my pencils were so sharp that year.

I haven't told anyone about my crush, though, not even Lara.

Todd lives one street over. Sometimes we play on his street, as a lot of kids from school live there. He's one of the smart kids who are in the enrichment program.

It's well known that a girl named Nicole Harris also has a crush on him. She's in the enrichment program as well. She's got it all. She's smart, cute, sensible, and is good at sports even though she's short. I hate being in the same group as her on sports day because I always come in second. At least in basketball I'm taller than her so still get to play center. I'm sure if she were taller, she'd bump me from the starting line.

We're friends and hang out now and again. She lives in a newer development in town, in a beautiful modern home that has a high, vaulted ceiling. *Both* her parents drive sports cars. She and her sister have canopy beds, and they share an adjoining bathroom. They remind me of Jessica and Elizabeth in the Sweet Valley High books.

It's Nicole's twelfth birthday and she's having a sleepover, and ten of us girls are invited. Lara's mom is so strict that she won't even allow her to sleep over at Nicole's house. She's going to pick her up at 9:30 p.m.

The party is in the unfinished basement of their house. Her parents order us pizza. Then we have cake and she opens presents.

We're all dancing to "Everybody Have Fun Tonight" by Wang Chung. It's such a fun song. When it ends, "Walk Like an Egyptian" by the Bangles comes on. A girl named Taylor breaks out and does the Egyptian walk, and we all laugh.

Suddenly a girl named Jen starts screaming and laughing. Taylor dances even sillier, thinking the laughter is for her.

The rest of us follow Jen's finger—some boys from school are outside the window!

Now we're all shrieking.

We run to the window and open it.

They're huddled in a pack, craning their necks to peek inside the window to see what we're doing.

"You girls dancing, can we join you?" the leader of the group, Donny, says.

We all giggle.

Everyone is talking and laughing at once.

Nicole suddenly turns serious and tells the boys, "You guys have to leave now. My parents will hear you. Sorry, guys, you gotta go!"

She reaches to close the window and adds, "Thanks for stopping by." Then draws the curtains.

I'm impressed by Nicole's maturity. I admire it. It's so different from what I would have done. I probably would have snuck the boys in or gone out the window to join them, like a little hooligan.

We try pretending we're not bummed that the boys had to leave.

"Go enjoy some snacks," Nicole says in an attempt to improve the mood of the room. Like snacks somehow make up for no boys.

Some girls go and load up on the candies and chips spread out on a side table, and others stand around the stereo that has now been turned down, looking for something to play. The fun energy from earlier went out the window with the boys.

Not long after, Nicole's mom walks downstairs. Lara's mom is behind her. The girls at the sleepover are all white. I'm the only Native. They all eagerly greet her. "Hi, Mrs. J." I have never called Lara's mom that.

They start to plead with her to let Lara stay. "Can Lara please sleep over? We're all having so much fun."

I don't join in. I already know *Mrs. J.* won't budge.

We all say goodbye to Lara. Nicole's mom tells us we should get ready for bed.

"We will. Good night, Mrs. Harris," the girls say in unison.

We all brought our own sleeping bags. Nicole says, "Mia, let's set up our sleeping bags beside each other."

We get into pyjamas and sit on our blankets, chatting about the boys and telling scary stories. Tracy, who became friendly with us after the bullying incident, starts telling a ghost story. Everyone else is hanging on her every word. But she lost me when parts of the story didn't seem realistic. I wander over to the snacks.

I start thinking about the boys. Todd wasn't with them—he doesn't hang out with that crowd. My thoughts are quickly interrupted by the girls squealing at the end of Tracy's story. I rejoin them and let out a fake screech as well.

Soon, one by one, everyone starts falling asleep.

Except for me and Nicole. We stay up, whispering back and forth. "Who do you have a crush on?" she asks.

How can I tell her that I have a crush on the same person as her? "I don't have a crush on anyone right now," I say.

"Come on, you must like someone," she prods.

She keeps bugging me. And I don't know how, but she eventually gets it out of me.

"I like Todd," I whisper.

"I knew it!" She smiles knowingly.

She knew? What? Had I gazed at him longer than I should have? Does *anyone else* know?

We start giggling and sharing Todd stories. I start with the pencil sharpener back in fifth grade. Then she comes up with the idea that we should send him an anonymous love letter from a secret admirer. She quietly creeps upstairs to get paper and a pen.

We start with *Dear Todd, I'm a secret admirer.*

Nicole comes up with the next line—*I see you in the hall, because you're so tall.*

Todd *is* tall! We quietly laugh at our poetic brilliance.

After finishing the letter, we make a plan. Nicole will slip the note into Todd's jacket in the cloakroom on Monday since they are in the same class.

We start nodding off, barely able to whisper "good night."

The following week I wait patiently for a reply. Nothing. On Friday I bump into Nicole in the hall. "Well? Did you do it? Have you heard anything?" I ask.

She looks at me like she doesn't have a clue what I'm talking about.

"The letter!" I almost stomp my foot to emphasize my words.

"Ohh," she says with a smile. "I ended up telling him it was us. That we wrote the letter."

"WHAT?" I can't believe it. No big deal for her, because everyone already knows she likes him. My crush was a secret. It was the reason we said *secret* admirer. "What did he say?"

"He just chuckled. I gotta run, though. Catch up with you later, okay?" She takes off.

I decide I had better let Lara know. On the way home from school I say, "So, there's something I haven't told you…"

Lara's nodding, letting me know I have her full attention.

"I have a crush on Todd." I say it fast, like I'm trying to beat the basketball buzzer clock.

"*What?*" Lara blurts out. Then she starts laughing. "Mia, he's so funny-looking!"

"He is not!" I immediately regret telling her.

And she's one to talk. She's liked Todd's best friend Josh on and off for years, and he's totally goofy.

"Okay, you're right, he's not funny-looking. But he is tall. Since when?"

I tell her about Nicole's sleepover and the secret love letter. "And now he knows! Nicole told him *we* wrote the letter!"

"*What?*" Lara's mouth hangs open. She's as shocked as I was.

When we get to Lara's place we go straight to her room and close the door. She puts on a mixed tape and says she wants to know more. Like what I am going to do next.

What? Am I supposed to "do" something?

The following week Nicole and I are hanging out on Todd's street. I am still a bit annoyed with her about spilling my secret, but she doesn't seem to notice. The boys are riding down a hill on skateboards. Nicole and I borrowed boards, and we ride sitting on our butts.

I'm having so much fun. I forget about upsetting things like my terrible grades at school, my mom's drinking or that Grandma was in the hospital recently. We run back up the hill for the umpteenth time and are on our boards, ready to barrel down the hill. That's when Nicole says, "You're so pretty. What is your secret?"

I blink, snapping out of my fun daze. "What?"

My reaction must throw Nicole off. She fumbles for words and says, "I meant your skin is so nice. What kind of cream do you use?"

"Jergens," I say and take off down the hill on my board.

I feel irritated. I don't like that kind of attention. I'm wearing a new white hoodie that says *Lake Tahoe*. I'm wearing it because my mom bought it for me on her recent vacation. I use Jergens because there's a big tub of it on the bathroom sink. I'm grateful to wake up for school on time most days and to find clean clothes to wear. I don't try to be *pretty*.

And why is Nicole, with the beautiful home and walk-in closet, asking me what my secret is?

The next day at school, Todd's best friend Josh tells Lara that *Todd likes me too!*

Lara tells me at lunchtime, and we both quietly screech with delight.

News about Todd and me spreads quickly through school. I feel unprepared for it. Cal, a Native boy in my class that Lara and I both had crushes on over the years, says to me, "I hear you're going out with Todd."

I respond with a blank stare and walk away.

Lara, Josh, Todd and I are going on a double date this Saturday. Todd didn't ask me. Communication went from Todd to Josh and through to Lara. Todd and I haven't spoken since he officially revealed that he "likes me," even though we've always chatted casually as friends.

He'd ask me things like, "Hey, Mia, how many A's did you get on your report card?"

Was he crazy? I'd never gotten an A in my life!

"Three," I had replied. *Three?* Lying was becoming my new normal. But how could I have told him the truth? *I didn't get any As, Todd. In fact, I got Ds and Fs. How's your day going?*

Everything is getting so confusing.

It's Saturday, the day of our double date. My mom got her income tax refund, so she takes me shopping for a new coat. And gets me a Gore-Tex jacket! It was over two hundred dollars. It's a deep fuchsia pullover with a grey stripe across the front. It's so gorgeous!

Then we go to Rodhos for dinner. My mom orders a steak and I get a small pepperoni pizza. I tell her a bunch of kids from school are going to the movies later. I do not say it's a date! Sheesh! I would never tell her something like that. I try not to think about things too much or I'll start to get nervous.

Things like Nicole and I both like Todd, yet he chose me.

The theater is one block from the restaurant. I meet Lara there. "Your jacket!" she exclaims. "It's *so* cool!"

I'm telling her all about my shopping trip when a car pulls up. Todd is in the front seat, so I assume it's his mother dropping them off. Josh climbs out of the back seat.

We say our hellos and walk inside.

Todd goes first and stands at the ticket window. "Two tickets for *Police Academy 3*," he says.

The lady behind the counter takes his money and slides the tickets under the glass. He turns and hands me a ticket.

It's my first date, so I'm not sure what to expect. I thank him and feel glad I left my five-dollar bill in my pocket.

Lara and I exchange looks.

As I start walking up the stairs, I overhear Josh say, "One ticket, please."

We find our seats. Josh chooses an aisle seat, Todd sits one seat away from him, leaving a spot for Lara, and I take a seat beside Todd.

Then Lara says to me, "I'll sit on the other side of you," leaving the seat beside Josh empty.

I sense her annoyance, so I say, "Let's go to the washroom before it starts."

As we enter the washroom, Lara shrieks, "He's such a loser! I had to pay for my own ticket!"

No one talks about money. But it occurs to me that maybe Josh didn't have enough money to buy her ticket. I don't share these thoughts, as I don't think Lara would understand. Instead I say, "Didn't I tell you he's goofy?"

"I can't believe I ever liked him," Lara says while teasing her bangs with her fingers in front of the mirror. She's wearing a pretty light-pink blouse and dangly multi-colored shell earrings.

"Well, in all fairness, you haven't liked him since last year," I say, staring at my Gore-Tex in the reflection.

"True," she says, reaching into her pocket for her lip balm. "I guess we're mostly here for you guys." She points her finger at me and, smiling, adds, "And your jacket!"

We grab popcorn and drinks and head back to our seats. I take off my jacket and lay it over the seat in front of me.

"Nice coat, Mia," Josh says. "Aren't those, like, really expensive?"

"Thank you. My mom just bought it for me." I smile.

The lights go out as the screen curtains open. I can't think of anything except Todd sitting beside me! But I don't like how things have been weird between us. I'm suddenly shy and he's quieter. Not a good combo!

The screen brightens on a scene, and I glance at my jacket. Just then Todd reaches for my hand. I manage to remain calm, act like it's no big deal. An everyday moment for Mia—doot-doot-doo.

I can hardly focus on the movie. Josh laughs throughout while shoveling popcorn into his face. Todd's hands are bigger than mine. He's lightly pinching my fingertips between his thumb and index finger. It's distracting, in an already awkward moment, yet kind of endearing. It's like we're old-timers, a couple.

The next few weeks are a blur. Nicole is no longer as friendly to me, which bothers me since we'd always been friends. And for what? Todd and I continue our new arrangement of mostly not talking.

Things eventually fizzle out between us, thank God, because I do not feel anywhere near ready for the world of dating.

Dance Recital

All those rainy walks to jazz class eventually pay off. For the end of the season we're putting on a show at the Performing Arts Center. Half the town bought tickets to watch.

Our costumes are pink bodysuits with matching tights. Our dance instructor had parents sew on shiny black-sequin strands across the body, with a bow at the top.

We're getting ready to leave home—I'm already wearing my costume. I'm disappointed Grandma's not coming to watch, but I do a couple of twirls for her in the living room before we go.

She nods and smiles slightly with her eyes.

The dressing room at the center has vanity mirrors lined with light bulbs. It's just like on television. We're all wearing a lot of makeup as part of our costumes. "Isn't this exciting!" someone says as she stares at her reflection, applying red lipstick.

"It *is*!" I say.

There is still time before we perform, so I wander around backstage. It's dark, and I can hardly see anything. The girl was right—this is exciting. No one is around, so I decide to do a joyous little leap.

On landing, I smash my shin into something. It hurts so badly, but I have to force myself not to cry because I don't want to ruin my makeup. I lean forward to put pressure on my leg and try to make the throbbing stop. I see what I hit my shin on—a wooden speaker painted black to be unseen on stage. It's unseen, all right.

"Mia!" I hear my instructor call out.

We are up next, so I join my group, and we make our way to enter stage right. We take our places behind the curtain. I can hear the audience shuffling in their seats. I hope my family can see me from where they are sitting. My mom, Aunt Lorraine and Uncle Jerry are here to watch.

The stage lights in my face are blinding. I put my chin up, focus my eyes straight ahead and smile, waiting for the cue. The curtains slowly open and loud music begins to boom from the speakers.

When we begin, there's no time to think about anything, I'm so in the moment. My focus is always on my next step and keeping time. I suddenly see the reason we went over our routine week after week.

Our performance is flawless, and we get a standing ovation at the end. From the back row, farthest left on the stage, I'm beaming.

Worst News and Even Worse News

We've just finished sixth grade. Lara's mom has decided to transfer her and her brother back to the private school they attended before moving to our school in fourth grade.

Lara has been getting into trouble at school with other girls. I don't know how things happen, they just do. Over the past few months, she has been in the principal's office several times for fighting.

Sometimes I was the bad influence. One time I talked her into skipping class. I got the idea from my older cousin. She said they do it at high school all the time. So that's what Lara and I did. Instead of returning to school after lunch, we hid at a park.

When her mom got the call after school, oh boy, was she in trouble. The final straw was the day a teacher told us to hurry back to class after the lunch bell rang. We weren't moving fast enough, so he snapped at us to move it. When he turned to walk away, Lara stuck her middle finger up at him. Another student saw and tattled on her. She got suspended for it.

Lara's a good student. She gets all As and Bs. She has a desk in her bedroom where she does her homework right after school. I'm not allowed over to her house until she's done. Once in a while her mom will let us do homework together, mostly when we say we have a project to work on.

I am not a serious student. When I get home, I look for a snack and then join Grandma for whatever she's watching on television. My grades have been consistently slipping since the beginning of fifth grade.

There's usually so much going on at our house that I tend to get distracted, forget I have homework or misplace it. I miss a lot of school too, especially on Mondays after we've gone for a weekend getaway. My mom and her siblings have so much fun drinking and partying that they enjoy themselves to the last minute. We arrive back home Sunday nights at 11:00 p.m. (almost on the dot). By the time I help my mom to bed, get her shoes and glasses off and go to sleep myself, it's midnight.

This usually results in my sleeping in the next day. I head in to school after the morning recess break or else I don't make it at all. When I walk into the living room in the morning, around 10:00 a.m., Grandma's awake. She'll snap her eyes at me, disappointed that I'm late for school yet again.

One time I went to school at recess and everyone was lined up at the water fountain, getting a drink after PE.

When Lara saw me, she glared at me! Probably because I hadn't shown up at our meeting spot and left her waiting to walk to school together.

Lara telling me she has to move to another school is the worst news. But then I get even worse than that.

I've failed sixth grade.

When I get my report card at the end of the day, I head straight to the washroom. I go into an empty stall, open my report card and read it. Ds and Fs, right down the entire column. My eyes quickly scan the writing until I read the dreaded words from Mrs. Allen—*Mia will need to repeat sixth grade*. I read it three times. It gets worse each time.

It is beyond humiliating. Horrifying, like someone startled me and that scared feeling is lodged in my body. I stand in the stall, stunned. I can't bear the thought of facing my classmates.

On our walk home from school, Lara says, "I got four As and the rest Bs. How about you?"

How do you share failure? How do you tell your best friend, who is smart, assertive, a good dancer, has *decorative throw pillows, for crying out loud*, that you failed sixth grade?

You don't.

"My mom told me not to open my report card until I got home," I say. Then I quickly change the subject.

After my mom reads my report card, she phones the school principal and sets up a meeting to discuss my options. Could I take summer school? The principal refers us to the school district's head office. After a few attempts, my mom finally connects with someone. They tell her there is no summer school for elementary grades.

The embarrassment that has been lodged in my body since the bathroom stall eventually starts to fade. It's more waves that wash over me now and again. I have no plans to tell Lara about failing. As we head into summer, I do my best not to think about it.

Mary Moves Out

The only person I feel comfortable telling I failed sixth grade is Mary. She responds by saying, "Miaaa," drawn out in a tone that is a gentle *shame on you*.

Yet it doesn't make me feel bad. It is more of a relief to get it out.

I don't remember when Mary came to live with us. Or when foster care placed her here. She's been here as far back as I can remember. Maybe when I was two or three? She's under Grandma's care, and they share a bedroom. She's Christian like Grandma too. Except when Grandma switches to different churches, Mary stays at the Native Pentecostal. She likes it there and has made a lot of good friends.

Mary calls Grandma "Big Mom" like everyone else. But Mary kind of seems like an outsider in our family. She's part of it but not.

She babysits me and my cousins all the time. We often give her a hard time or play pranks. We say things like,

"You have toe jams" or tease her about her crush on the church leader's son. She gets mad at us, saying, "You kids are nothing but brats! Rotten brats!"

But if we ever feel we actually hurt her feelings, we rush to her side and apologize. We genuinely love and care for Mary. She doesn't have a mean bone in her body. In no time, though, we are back to our childish antics, like snapping her bra strap.

Grandma does all the cooking and Mary does all the dishes. She does other chores as well. She's always doing homework from high school and likes to watch TV and eat sunflower seeds. My mom's not nice to Mary at times, yelling at her and stuff. She yells at me too, but not as much as at Mary. One time when I was in first grade, Mary and I were running late for school because I couldn't find my other shoe. This made my mom mad, and she hunted under the stairs for my shoe (which I'd hidden behind the trunk because I didn't want to go to school). When she found it, she threw it toward us so hard that it went right past us and hit the paned window, smashing the glass. We stood stunned, then Mary scurried over, grabbed my shoe and quickly put it on my foot. Then out the door we went.

One day, when I arrive home after sleeping at Lara's, I discover Mary is gone. Moved out, gone. Grandma seems very upset. Her eyes look different, like there's no one there. I've never seen her look like that before.

I can see my mom is mad. I don't know if there has been a disagreement or what happened. No one is saying anything, and I don't dare ask, but just like that, Mary's gone.

Mary had just graduated high school. I attended her graduation ceremony by myself. No one else in our family went. She looked so pretty in her peach strapless dress, and her grad partner looked nice in his suit. I was beaming with pride for her in the audience. I love Mary yet have never said those words to her.

Heck, none of us have said it. Grandma's never once told me she loves me. I know she does, of course, but we don't talk about those kinds of things.

Not long after Mary moves out, I hear she's working at the donut shop, so I decide to go and see her.

I take a seat on a stool at the counter. I don't say anything. I just stare at her with a look that says, *What, you're just going to leave without saying goodbye?*

My energy speaks loud and clear. As Mary busies herself behind the counter, in her orange-and-brown uniform, her back is toward me, so she glances over her shoulder and says, "I moved in with friends, Mia. And I'm happy there."

"Do you like working here?" I ask, as if the past is far behind us.

"Yeah, it's a job," she replies.

"Do you get free donuts?"

Mary laughs and turns to me with a "*Shh!*" then adds, "My boss is in the back."

I don't stay long. I don't even order a donut.

When I turn to leave, Mary says, "Mia." And slides a glazed donut to me.

I pop in to see her when I'm in the area, and things between us kinda go back to normal. Sometimes I walk in and she'll say, "It's busy right now." Those days I turn around and walk right back out the door.

Soccer Camp

Lara and I signed up for summer soccer camp. A tournament is being held in Prince George this weekend. It's about a nine-hour drive from Prince Rupert. We're both going, and get this—it's without parents! We can hardly believe it.

We decide to dress the same for the trip. We both purchased Tour de France T-shirts from Fields last week and decide to wear those, with black stretch pants and matching purses.

Her parents drive us to the pickup spot.

A couple of buses are traveling together. Everyone's standing around waiting to board the bus. Travel bags are scattered on the ground waiting to be loaded. Lara and I go and look for our coach to check in.

When we get back, I see Jeff Roberts, the cute boy from Kitkatla that we prank called. I'd forgotten about him.

He's sitting on my duffel bag!

He's wearing a white sweatshirt that says *Haida Gwaii Watchmen*. The same kind the pretty girl at the basketball tournament was wearing. It's not uncommon for Natives to be from two different Nations.

He's chuckling with a buddy. Then he leans off my bag, looks at the tag and says, "Who's Mia Douglas?"

I want the ground to swallow me up. "That's me, it's my bag," I manage.

"Hope you don't mind me sitting on it," he says.

"That's fine." I wave my hand casually.

Lara's oblivious to what's happening because she doesn't know that it's *him*, and is more bothered that her parents are lingering. She's motioning to them that they can leave, mouthing *Bye!* with her lips.

We load the bus and choose seats in the middle section. We can hardly contain our excitement. Lara shrieks, "No parents!" then adds, "Oh yeah, my parents." We look out the window, and they're still there. The bus engine starts to roar, and we wave a final goodbye as we depart.

I notice Jeff is not on the bus. Instead, he's walking away from it. Maybe he was seeing a friend off.

We make our way along a familiar stretch of Highway 16. Kids get up and start visiting with one another. A Native boy sitting in front of us turns around. He's leaning on his knees staring at us and says, "Why are you guys dressed the same?"

"Because we're cool," Lara replies sharply.

"Oh." He seems satisfied with her response and turns back around.

Lara elbows me discreetly in the side and we chuckle.

We dig into our snacks and start planning what we'll do when we get there and, of course, what we'd like to buy at the mall.

Lara and I requested to be billeted at the same home. After our hosts pick us up, we eat dinner together at their place. They seem nice enough. Then they show us to a camper in the driveway. Lara and I elbow each other to express our excitement at being in a camper. We thank our host and say good night as she leaves.

"A freakin' camper!" Lara shrieks.

"Way cooler than being inside," I add.

We get into our pyjamas, fold down the double bed we will be sharing, turn the lights out and settle in for the night. We giggle and talk about the highlights of the day. I finally get to tell her about Jeff Roberts sitting on my bag. She is disappointed that I didn't show her who he was.

"We'd better go to sleep. The tournament starts early," Lara says, and just like that, she turns over and is fast asleep.

I can't seem to unwind. And besides, it's only 9:30 p.m. I never go to sleep this early at home. I lie awake for close to an hour before eventually falling asleep.

The games are held on a huge field. We win our first game, so we get to spend the next few hours watching other Prince Rupert teams play and eating food from the concession stand. Still riding high from our first win. Our next game is at 3:00 p.m. and we're playing a local team. We have to win that game in order to play a third.

The opposing team dominates us from the start. The teams are co-ed. Our team captain has the ball and is making his way down the field when he yells to our teammates, "Pick up a man!" He seems frustrated.

We lose the game 4–1. I play defense, and even though I spent most of the time on the bench, it's still a devastating loss.

Lara is even more bummed about losing. "This sucks," she says as we change out of our cleats.

"It does," I reply, putting my cleats in my backpack.

We hang out, chatting with other players from our team. Then we decide to make our way toward the mall, which is within walking distance.

I quickly forget about our loss, as I am excited to go shopping. The mall in Prince George is four times the size of ours. I've been many times with my family, so I'm familiar with the layout.

I make my way in and out of stores that I like while Lara mopes along behind me. I tire of her gloominess. "What's the big deal?" I ask while looking through a clothing rack. "We've lost tournaments before."

She moves to block me. "Didn't you see my breakaway? If I'd made the shot, it would have gotten us that much closer to a win!"

Ah, now I understand. "That was awesome. I was cheering for you from the bench."

"But I didn't make the shot," she mumbles, turning away.

"A lot of people missed. Our captain missed an important goal." I stop to look at her. "You played your best. Now cheer up. We're in Prince George. At a freakin' mall!"

"You're right." Her spirits start to lift.

I think of the food court. "Are you hungry? Maybe eating will make you feel better. Or an ice cream!" I do jazz hands. I never do jazz hands. I shove my hands into my pockets and lead the way to the food court.

Lara smiles and follows my lead.

After eating slices of pizza and getting ice cream, Lara's mood improves. We continue shopping and each buy a couple of pairs of slouchy socks and earrings. And I buy a peach-colored tank top, which I change into in the washroom right away.

After returning home, Lara and I both agree the soccer trip was a highlight of summer!

Two Minutes in Heaven

Lara's mom must feel guilty about moving her to a new school because she lets Lara throw an end-of-summer party in their rec room.

Lara and I make a list of classmates to invite from school—even a few boys! We make a cool mixed tape, and her mom buys a bunch of snacks for the party.

At first Lara's mom hangs around. She sits on the couch with a weird smile plastered to her face while she watches us dance. With boys! It's so awkward.

As soon as she goes upstairs, we decide to play a game called Two Minutes in Heaven that we learned about from the book *Are You There God? It's Me, Margaret* by Judy Blume.

You go into a closet or washroom with a boy and you are supposed to kiss. I was selected to go with Cal, the Native boy Lara and I used to like.

We are standing in front of the sink, facing each other with the lights off. I immediately feel nervous. I've never kissed a boy before. And Cal is my friend! When he moves toward me, I back up. He moves again, and I back up again. Then he chuckles and whispers, "If you're too scared to kiss, we could just say we did."

"Okay!" I say, so relieved.

When we walk out of the washroom, everyone asks if we kissed.

We both smile slyly, nodding like we did.

I am grateful to Cal for that. Especially when, the following day, Lara tells me the boy she went in the washroom with stuck his tongue in her mouth. She says it was the most disgusting thing, like a lizard.

Back to School

It's the first day of school. The feelings of dread and humiliation have returned. I did my best to block out failing sixth grade over the summer. I never told anyone.

Lara having moved to another school is now more of a relief. Her finding out I failed is one less thing I need to worry about.

As I get closer to the school, I sense that not even my stonewashed designer-brand back-to-school clothes can save me.

I am assigned to a split grades-six-and-seven class. Things could be worse. I could have been in a grade-six-only class where it would be immediately obvious I failed. At least in a split class I can blend in.

When we enter our new classroom, our teacher is standing at the front of the room. Her name is written on the blackboard—Mrs. Flett. She's an attractive older woman, tall, slim and blond. She keeps one hand casually in her pants pocket while standing in front of our class.

It's a confident-looking pose. Even though my spirits are low, I can tell I'm going to like her.

"Sixth graders on the right, seventh graders on the left," she says. She indicates the divide by waving her arm down a middle aisle.

I choose a seat closer to the front, in a sixth-grade row right next to the seventh graders, hoping no one will notice.

Cal immediately says, "Mia, what are you doing over there? Seventh graders are over here."

He assumes I have misunderstood the instructions. The idea of me failing hasn't entered his mind.

I glance over at him in the next row, a seventh-grade row, and then slowly turn back and stare at the chalk-board.

"Hey," he says. He's lowered his voice.

I look over at him.

He leans toward me. "Did you fail or something?"

I wish that my seat could somehow swallow me up.

I can't answer him. I can't say the words *Yes, Cal, I failed*.

I know I failed. I've accepted it. But I also know I'm not *stupid*. I didn't fail because I'm not smart enough.

The teacher asks for everyone's attention.

Throughout the day a few other classmates ask me why I am sitting in the sixth-grade section. I answer no one. I barely speak all day. My only consolation is that my enrichment program friends like Nicole and Todd are in the seventh-grade-only class. Even though we aren't as close as we used to be, I still hope they don't find out I failed.

At the end of the week, I'm walking from the gymnasium when I see Nicole in the main hallway. She's standing looking at the class lists.

As I get closer, she turns to me and whispers, "Mia, did you *fail* sixth grade?"

Her whisper somehow lessens the humiliating blow.

My smart, good-at-everything friend Nicole. There is such shock in her tone that the only acceptable response I feel I can provide is "No."

Nicole glances back at the list with my name clearly displayed under grade six, as if telling me to look at what she's looking at.

I don't look. I've seen it already.

"I have a few assignments I need to finish up," I answer casually, almost confidently. But inside, I feel sick.

Changes

There's always so much change in our household. Not long after Mary moved out, my aunt and uncle and their two kids moved back to town from Vancouver, and now they're staying with us. I'm back to sharing a room with my mom again.

I sign up for jazz dance again this year. However, I also spend a lot of time with my older cousin Tonya. She's so cool. She smokes, swears and hangs out at the video arcade. I start missing dance classes so often that it seems there's no point in returning. I have lost all interest.

Of course, I get an earful for wasting my mom's money.

My mom doesn't like having her brother and his family at our home. She spends most of her time in our shared bedroom and even starts talking about us moving out and getting an apartment of our own. The idea of an apartment appeals to me a lot. I know a few people who live in them. I've lived my entire life in our house, though, and if we moved, I wouldn't see Grandma every day. I would miss her way too much, and I know she'd miss me.

Broken Glass

Lara's attending another school isn't as bad as we thought. We tell ourselves it's like being in different classes. We still hang out after school and on weekends as much as we always have.

I like hearing about her new friends from school. The two girls she hangs out with are named Sophia and Chloe. Lara says she'll have them over soon so that I can meet them. It sounds like another world over there, a Catholic private school. They wear navy blue uniforms. She also has a new crush. This time it's an Italian boy named Marco. He's all she's been talking about.

We're hanging out in Lara's room. She has a blown-glass figurine of horses pulling a carriage that she bought in Disneyland. She keeps it on top of her jewelry box even though it's a delicate piece that has to be moved on and off several times a day for her to get to her jewelry.

I go to lift it, as I have many times before, but this time the whole thing falls apart.

We both just stand there, shocked.

Lara calls her father, as there's broken glass to be cleaned up. After Lara explains what happened, her father looks at me like I wrecked it on purpose.

I would never do such a thing. I love Lara's room and all the nice things in it. It's where we spend most of our time.

But I do often break or wreck things. It's always accidental, of course. Things just happen.

One time I sat on a swivel chair in a department store and spun it around, not realizing a display case filled with crystalware was behind it until, along with the rest of the store, I heard a thunderous sound of smashing glass.

I froze for a moment, then quickly made my way through the store toward the changeroom, darting in between rows of clothes. My mom was with her sister Elsie, who was trying on wedding dresses.

The look on my face must have given me away. My mom whispered, "Mia, was that you?"

I answered only by widening my eyes further.

Just then my aunt came out of the changeroom wearing a stunning ivory lace wedding dress. She saw the look on our faces and, without saying a word, returned to the dressing room to change.

Within minutes the three of us fled the department store like bandits.

I feel bad about breaking Lara's ornament. Her dad puts the broken pieces onto a tray and sets it on top of the jewelry box. He says he will glue it back together later. It sits as a constant reminder of what I have done.

A Miracle and Other Disasters

It's a dreary Monday morning at the beginning of October. Mrs. Flett asks me to follow her to the book-storage room adjacent to our classroom.

I worry I have done something wrong.

When we get there she says, "Take a seat."

She leans against a table, facing me. "I don't know why you failed sixth grade. You clearly know what you're doing and are capable of doing the work. I'm going to have you start doing grade-seven work now."

"Okay," I say. It's the only reply I can muster.

A sense of relief washes over me.

She continues speaking, and I nod along.

I wasn't expecting this. My mind is racing, and a heavy weight lifts. I think back to the fib I'd told Nicole about having some assignments to finish up. Now maybe that won't be such a lie. And I won't have to worry about Lara finding out I failed. That is a huge relief.

"You will need to work hard to catch up, Mia. But I know you can do it." Mrs. Flett is looking me in the eye very seriously, but she's being kind and supportive too.

"I will," I assure her, holding her gaze.

And I do. I throw myself into Social Studies because it's a subject I like. We are learning about Egyptians. I also ask Mrs. Flett if I should move my desk over a row, to the seventh-grade row. She says it's fine where it is.

A few weeks later we get a substitute teacher. She announces she'll be with us for the entire week. Everyone likes having a substitute because we horse around and don't do as much work.

The following week we get another substitute and an announcement that Mrs. Flett will not be returning. We're not surprised, as before she left she had told us a bit about her health issues. But we are sad, as we all liked her. Me especially.

The next week I arrive to class and I see Mrs. Allen standing in our classroom.

The Mrs. Allen. The-one-who-failed-me Mrs. Allen. After we settle in, she informs us that she will be replacing Mrs. Flett as our teacher permanently.

I don't know what to think or feel. Other than her failing me and being moody at times, I've never necessarily had *problems* with her.

When she was our teacher last year, everyone else seemed to like her. She let girls style her hair while she sat at her desk and would update us weekly on her favorite television show, *LA Law*. She also liked Lara and paid special attention to her clothes.

We are seated at our desks after lunch. Mrs. Allen is at the front of the room, sitting on top of an empty desk, facing us. "Seventh graders," she says, "take out your Social Studies textbooks."

I reach for my textbook. It has a sphinx on the cover. I place it on top of my desk.

It immediately catches Mrs. Allen's eye. "Mia, what are you doing with a seventh-grade textbook—I failed you!" She practically yells it.

I freeze.

Several students jump to my defense. Cal takes the lead, and with a force equal to Mrs. Allen's says, "She does seventh-grade work now!"

Mrs. Allen's slate-blue eyes pierce through me. Like her way is the right way, and how dare anyone tell her different.

Cal is half standing, half sitting at his desk like a referee, ready.

Mrs. Allen's face is small and narrow, her lips thin and pursed. She gets up and walks toward the chalkboard. "Everyone open to chapter ten."

Log Jumping

My friends at school this year are all over the place. I don't hang around with any specific group since Lara moved schools. I'm like a floater, which is fine by me.

I went log jumping with some kids from school yesterday. We went down to the harbor where a bunch of logs were tied together. You jump from one log to the next. You have to be fast and keep moving because the logs sink when you land on them. I just watched at first because I was too scared to try, but once I did, it was so fun!

Well, until the police showed up.

Boy, were they mad at us. They said it was very dangerous and that a girl had drowned doing exactly what we were doing. They said if we fell into the water, we would be trapped under the logs.

I told them I was a strong swimmer and I had been in swimming lessons for years.

That angered one policeman even more. He pointed to the logs floating in the harbor and said, "When you unexpectedly fall into the cold water, you panic. Do you think you'd know which direction to swim to try to come out from under the logs?"

They ended up taking us to the police station and called our parents.

When they called my house, Grandma answered. The police officer said, "This is Constable Boyd of the RCMP. We have Amelia down at the station."

Grandma hung up on Constable Boyd.

I told him it must have been my grandmother and that she is hard of hearing. She doesn't speak much English either, I added.

When I got home and told my mom what happened, she laughed about Grandma hanging up on the police and then told me not to go on the logs ever again.

MTV Music Video

Lara is still in jazz. She loves everything dance and was disappointed when I told her I had quit.

We're hanging out in her rec room one day when she says, "Choose a song and let's make up a music video." We love watching them on MTV.

"How about 'Money for Nothing,' by Dire Straits?" I had "borrowed" the tape from Uncle Dan's room and brought it to Lara's.

"Let's do it." She's already trying out dance moves in the middle of the room.

We decide that I will play the lead singer. Lara will be on electric guitar and we enlist Owen for drums. We improvise on equipment and do some rehearsing.

Lara leaves the room, tells me to press Play on the cassette and says she'll join us for her part.

I stand holding my mic as the slow intro begins. I start lip-syncing the words *I want my MTV...* Owen's on drums, and then comes the song's amazing guitar opening riff, which is Lara. She enters the room by flying across the floor on her knees while playing her brother's plastic guitar. Then she leans back as far as she can go while wildly strumming the guitar strings. Owen and I pick up on her energy and get into it as well.

We're so pumped. For our next run-through we decide I will throw fake money and fluffy little chicks left over from Easter, timed to the song's lyrics.

After that we feel we're ready to perform. Lara invites her parents to come down and watch.

They sit side by side on the couch.

I start to worry about my song selection, as it has some offensive language. Standing in front of her parents, their eyes locked on me, stage fright sets in. I suddenly wish our pretend stage had a pretend drop floor that could swallow me up. I nervously hold the mic. The intro seems to go on and on. My lips feel ten pounds each, but I manage to mouth the words. A sense of relief comes when Lara enters, flying across the floor on electric guitar. Totally unscripted, she adds to her performance by jumping on an armchair and then leaping off like she's Joan Jett.

She puts on an amazing and electrifying performance. Her parents stand up and applaud us, and say we all did an excellent job.

Visit from Mary

It's late spring. We had gotten word that Mary was pregnant. Not long after, we hear she's given birth to a baby boy.

Grandma and I are sitting at home when the telephone rings—it's Mary.

"Who is at the house right now?" Mary asks.

"Just me and Grandma," I reply.

"Your mom's not there?" Mary asks, all serious.

"No."

"Will your mom be coming home soon?" she adds.

"No," I answer, wondering what's with the twenty questions.

"Okay. I'm going to bring the baby to meet Big Mom," Mary says. "We'll take a cab now."

We hang up and I tell Grandma.

Her eyes light up, and she tells me to hurry and tidy the living room.

Within half an hour, Mary arrives with the baby and places him in Grandma's lap. Then she goes and sits on the couch. She seems nervous. It's the first time she's been to our house since she moved out. "His name's Joshua," she says proudly.

I go sit on the arm of Grandma's chair. "Ooh, he's so cute," I say. Grandma nods, smiling at the baby with her eyes.

I carry on cootchie-cooing to the baby. It's not hard, as he's a sweet little thing. He's a full-on white baby with blue eyes. Mary's fairer-skinned herself, but the baby's father has to be white. She doesn't mention who he is, and we don't ask.

I get to hold the baby too. I'm glad Mary brought him over. It's like she's letting Grandma know she still cares. He mostly sleeps during the visit, as newborns tend to do, and they don't stay long.

When Mary leaves, she gives Grandma a quick hug. I still don't know what happened the day Mary moved out. But I sense this visit is something they both needed.

Seventh-Grade Graduation

It's the day of our graduation. Everyone's super excited. There's going to be a ceremony and a dance afterward.

I borrow a black-and-white Esprit shirt from Tonya. I wear it with white pants and pointy flats. The top is big on me, but I don't care. It's so cool. She got it on a shopping trip to Vancouver on the May long weekend.

We're assembled in the gymnasium. They have us sitting up front like we're in a choir. After a short speech congratulating us, the principal calls our names and we each walk over to our teacher, who hands us our graduation certificate. Mrs. Allen shakes our hands and so does the principal. It's a fun formal occasion.

Afterward everyone's chatting in groups when a class-mate named Carrie points to my graduation certificate and says, "Yours isn't signed."

I look down and see that the principal has signed, but Mrs. Allen has not. Carrie's certificate has both signatures. I check another girl's—it has both.

I get a sinking feeling.

A celebratory mood fills the gymnasium. A *Congratulations* banner hangs above the stage, and another one says *Grad '87*. There are streamers and balloons throughout the gym, but I can't focus on anything other than my unsigned certificate.

What does it mean? Did I not pass seventh grade? Was I ever *in* seventh grade? My eyes follow Mrs. Allen around the room. The moment she's alone, I approach her and in a low voice ask, "What does it mean if you didn't sign my certificate?"

I hate myself for the nervousness in my voice. For how small I feel standing before her.

Her response doesn't help. She looks at me like I have some nerve asking her and responds, "Didn't I sign it?" Without looking at the certificate, she snatches it from me and walks away.

I watch her wiry frame disappear, I assume to go look for a pen.

The real graduates are having fun. Meanwhile, I feel the need for Pepto-Bismol.

Mrs. Allen returns, hands me the signed copy and says, "There," and walks away.

I make my way to the washroom—no one is in there. I take my time washing my hands. I linger, staring at my reflection in the mirror and at Tonya's striped shirt. I'm no longer in a celebratory mood but do my best to shrug off the feeling before rejoining my classmates.

I manage to go through the motions. The girls mostly dance in a group or hang out at the punch bowl. Only a handful of boys are comfortable enough to dance, so girls swarm them. I don't bother.

When the DJ plays "Nothing's Gonna Stop Us Now" by Starship, our seventh-grade graduation song, Cal walks over and asks me to dance. He single-handedly saves the evening from total disaster, the way you'd expect a good friend who'd stuck up for you over the years to do. I am grateful to him for that.

After the song ends, I go and call Tonya from the office and ask her to pick me up. She has her driver's license now!

When I leave the auditorium, I drop my graduation certificate into the trash.

Family Wedding

Family weddings are fun, and my cousin's wedding last night was no exception. I'd gotten a grown-up-looking dress to wear when we went to Prince George for the long weekend.

I danced with my cousins and uncles all night. It was so much fun. They had a live band play, and the musicians were total rock 'n' rollers, like Whitesnake. They had long hair, their shirts were unbuttoned down to their navels, and they drank beer right onstage.

The dance floor quickly filled when they sang "Lager and Ale" by Kim Mitchell. Everyone went nuts dancing, jumping up and down, arms raised over their heads. Even me! Well, kind of.

Grandma stays at dances until around 10:00 p.m. and then she goes home. She never dances, although once I did see her waltz at my aunt's wedding. It was part of the mother-and-son-in-law dance.

When the Kim Mitchell song ends, she waves me over and tells me that she is ready to go. I find a designated driver and we bring her home.

I decide to change into jeans and a T-shirt so I can be comfortable for the rest of the dance. I shake a dash of perfumed powder down the inside of my shirt. I catch Grandma watching me through my open bedroom door (I have my own room again).

I know she worries herself sick about me. She has already tried talking me into staying home, saying, "When people get drunk it's dangerous, and you shouldn't be out so late, Amelia!"

I don't listen to her. I'd rather be where my mom is so I can make sure she's okay. Grandma doesn't seem to understand that.

The dance ends at 1:00 a.m. We go to my aunt and uncle's afterward for a house party. It isn't unusual for me to be at such places. I often play bartender, replenishing drinks or clearing empties at family house parties. I'm also the DJ. I'm skilled at reading the mood of a room and adjusting the playlist accordingly. I can easily tell the difference between a Bob Seger or a Billy Joel crowd.

The next morning my family wakes up and starts "sipping," as they call it. The newlyweds are opening their beautifully wrapped wedding presents when a guy who is still tipsy from the night before falls on top of the gifts piled on the floor.

The bride gets upset and dashes off crying.

Then we get a phone call that Grandma is at the hospital because she fell getting off the bus this morning and broke her arm!

I feel sick. I immediately blame myself. I should have been with her. Instead I'm here with these drunken fools falling on top of wedding presents.

My uncle, who called to tell us, says they've just finished with Grandma's cast and he's taking her home.

I go straight to my mom and ask for money for a taxi.

When I arrive home, I burst through the door and see Grandma sitting in her armchair. My aunt and uncle are on the couch.

"Out partying all night with your mother?" my uncle's wife says. She always takes jabs at me like that.

I race to Grandma's side and give her a big squeeze. She seems fine, happy even, but I feel sick inside.

The next day Grandma is resting on the couch with her arm propped on a pillow. I grab my felt pens and decide to sign her cast. She's watching TV and not paying attention to me.

I hope you get better soon.

I love you SO much.

Love, Mia

I draw a bunch of colorful hearts as well.

I poke Grandma's side to show her my handiwork.

She gasps in shock and then laughs, saying, "Du wah, Amelia! Christian people aren't supposed to wear markings like that!"

Mine is the only signature on that cast she wears for eight weeks.

Rules

Lara has always had so many rules to follow. She can't play outside until she's done her homework, done practicing her lessons, finished her chores, or she has to be home by such and such a time. The list goes on and on.

My mom's given me a handful of weird rules to follow. I am not allowed to read comic books because she says they'll make me too lazy to read actual novels. I am not allowed to take fried-bologna sandwiches to school because only Indians and poor people eat them, and she always discourages me from going to the video arcade. I'm not exactly sure why.

I snuck there with Tonya once. It didn't seem that bad.

I'm heading into junior high, and it feels like going into the unknown. I suddenly wish I had a list of rules to follow. To-dos and not-to-dos for life. I sense it will be very different from elementary school, and I don't know if I'm ready.

Even my body is different now. I'm way more developed than most girls.

I know he was only kidding around, but toward the end of seventh grade, I caught Cal standing behind me in class, pretending like he was cupping my behind with his hands, then motioning to the boys about it.

I wasn't even aware of that part of my body in that way.

He seemed embarrassed that I'd caught him. I just walked away as if I hadn't seen anything.

What should I have done, though? Tattled to the teacher? Slapped him like women do in the movies? Cried like the white girls?

Rules. I could use some of those.

Boarding School

Now that I'm going into high school, it makes me think of the stories my mom shared of when she went from seventh grade to eighth. How different things were for her.

She grew up in Kitkatla, and their schooling system only went to grade seven. If you'd even call it learning. My mom said their non-Native teachers regularly mistreated and strapped them.

She said that after seventh grade, if you wanted to continue learning, you had to move away from the reserve. At twelve going on thirteen years old, she and her parents had to make the difficult decision—live the rest of her life with a seventh-grade education, or leave her home, family and community to graduate from high school?

My mom and one of her older sisters decided they wanted to graduate. The Canadian government billeted them at homes in Coquitlam—over 1,500 kilometers away from Kitkatla. They never understood why they were sent so far away when there was a high school in nearby Prince Rupert.

Yet there they found themselves. Placed into separate homes with ḵ'amkswiwaḥs, white people, who were not only strangers to them but whose way of life was different as well. She said no one prepared them for what life would be like living off-reserve. How could they?

Although eager to learn, they found the stress of adjusting to a new way of life, and the prejudices they faced at the mostly white high school in Coquitlam, too much to bear. My mom's older sister was the first to quit.

My mom stuck it out. But it wasn't easy. She was far from home and all alone. She got bounced from boarding home to boarding home until they eventually found a suitable fit with an older retired couple.

After five long years, my mom became the first person in her family to graduate from high school. She said she didn't merely get by, but received good marks.

I don't know if I would have been able to do that.

I wouldn't have lasted that long or being that far away from my family. Especially Grandma! And I probably wouldn't have been able to stand being mistreated either. Nobody should have to endure that. It makes me sad to think that my mom did.

Junior High

Tomorrow is the first day of junior high. I can't believe I'm in eighth grade! I'm nervous yet excited at the same time. Tonya said, "Don't bring your school supplies on the first day like you did in elementary school," adding, "You'll look like a total nerd." It's going on midnight, but I don't think I'll be able to sleep a wink!

For the first day, I wear khaki pants with the legs tightly rolled, a black fitted T-shirt with a pink flamingo on the breast pocket, and black pointy flats that I bought at Le Château.

For my thirteenth birthday, my mom gave me her West Coast carved Native pendant. It's so beautiful—it's the nicest thing she owned. I wasn't expecting it. I wear it proudly and admire the gold sheen in the mirror as I spray on perfume.

I pick up the phone and ring Lara to say I'm leaving and I'll meet her outside.

The high school is within walking distance of where we live, but we've given ourselves some extra time just in case. Lara went to the West Edmonton Mall for her summer trip and did a ton of shopping. She always has a lot of nice clothes. She's wearing a loose-fitting beige Au Coton outfit. It's a cool look that makes her seem older.

For some reason, she seems standoffish this morning, so I act the same. Maybe this is how high school students are supposed to act—chill.

We reach the main entrance of the school. There's an excited buzz in the air. The crowd of students assembled out front is overwhelming to me. I can't imagine how it will look when ninth and tenth graders show up.

This morning is a welcome for eighth graders only. Lara spots a group that is waving her over. I only recognize one person, a girl she's been hanging out with lately. We join them and I notice Lara's suddenly enthusiastic, laughing and much more talkative than she had been.

A teacher standing at the top of a staircase starts speaking to the crowd. He informs us that our homeroom numbers are posted in the main hallway, alphabetically under our last names. Everyone slowly shuffles toward the double doors. I notice a few students carrying bags filled with school supplies. I guess they didn't have an older cousin to warn them.

A brightly colored banner hangs overhead welcoming us, and multiple signs and arrows show us which way to go once we enter the building. Based on our last names, Lara and I are immediately separated.

During the last month of seventh grade, we'd had a one-day orientation at the high school. Unfortunately, I had missed school that day, so this is all new to me.

After finding my homeroom number, I make my way there. It is easy enough to find. I enter and look for a seat.

The room is already half full. I don't see anyone from my elementary school, which I find surprising. I recognize faces, of course, as we played other schools at various sporting events over the years. A lot of the students seem familiar with one another already.

The teacher arrives and introduces himself. I focus on his lazy eye. He has us go around the room introducing ourselves. It's more of an overview rather than a formal class. He gives us printouts of our class schedules, locker numbers and cherry-red agendas. "If you want to succeed," he says, "you must get into the habit of using an agenda. Any questions?"

A boy makes a joke, and a few kids join in laughing. Then the teacher dismisses us for the day.

I know there is no way I will find Lara in a crowd this size, so I decide to go and locate my locker.

Friendship Bracelets and Lockers

Lara and I have no memory of meeting. If I had to guess when our friendship started, I'd say we were five years old. In all those years, her room stayed exactly the same. The only thing that changed over the years was her bed quilt.

It's Friday morning, the end of our first week. I'm early picking Lara up for school, so I go and wait in her room—it's completely different. Lara and I have both been busy lately, but has it been that long since I've been to her place?

Her desk is gone and there's an armchair from their den in its place. There are now posters all over the wall and a framed picture of one of her new friends.

As we make our way to school, a silver bracelet slides down Lara's left wrist and catches my eye. I spot some lettering. "That's nice. What does it say?" I ask.

She twists her wrist upright so I can read it. It says *Jessica*. The name of the girl whose framed picture is on her wall.

"You borrowed her bracelet?" I ask.

"They're friendship bracelets," Lara replies. "We thought it would be fun to switch names—she has mine."

"Cool," I manage to get out.

Custom-made friendship bracelets. I had no idea they'd become *that* close of friends.

We finally arrive at school and make plans to meet by Lara's locker at lunch.

Junior high is so different. I like not knowing anyone in my classes—I feel like I've moved to a new town.

It is still a rush, though. After each bell rings, everyone spills into the hallway and heads off to yet another class. There aren't as many students looking lost, carrying schedules in their hands. Earlier in the week, I had to stop a teacher and ask for directions to my math class, which turned out to be on a different floor!

At lunch I make my way to Lara's locker. It's on the main floor by the library, across from the girls' washroom. It's a central location where clusters of students gather.

She arrives and unlocks her combination with one hand, like a pro.

"How were your classes?" I ask.

"Awesome." She tells me about friends in the same classes as her. "Bummer we don't have any classes together," she adds.

The "bummer" feels like an afterthought. Like she had to throw it in.

"Where's your locker?" she asks.

"Lower floor, near the back doors."

"WHAT?" Lara's mouth drops open. "Get out."

I stare and say nothing.

"Let's go see," she says, shutting her door and locking it.

We make our way down the double flight of stairs to what feels like a dark, depressing dungeon. I am embarrassed to take her here, as if we've crossed to the bad part of town.

The building is old. My locker area is deserted and lined with dinged-up navy blue lockers on each side. Lara's locker upstairs is newer and light beige.

At least there are other Native kids whose lockers are close to mine. I smile as I pass one of them.

My locker is steps from the doors leading to where the headbangers hang out. Lara hasn't said a word since we've come downstairs. Suddenly she says, "Mia, you can't stay down here."

She's not looking at the surroundings. She's staring at me, as if I need convincing. "This is terrible. It's so dark down here! And that's where the smokers hang out," she says, pointing at the double doors with her index finger.

"Don't you think I know?" I say, frustrated as I concentrate on the combination lock, making sure I get the number right.

I open the door and look up at her. "This is where I'm assigned. What am I supposed to do?"

We stare at each other, silent.

"Come share my locker!" Lara blurts out.

I'm used to her quick ways, but I wasn't expecting her to come up with that.

"Gather your stuff, quick," she says.

We clear out my locker and she helps me carry my things. "Let's get outta here!" Lara whispers, like we're a couple of bandits. Then we make our way back upstairs to where all the action and decent lighting seem to be.

Since we don't have any classes together, it's fun sharing a locker. We see each other briefly between classes when we exchange textbooks. But we have to continually work at staying organized, because lockers are not meant for sharing.

The following months of high school are a blur. Picture day comes and goes. Lara's mom likes my picture so much she asks if she can have one to put on their fireplace mantel. Lara laughs and tells her mom not to be weird.

By the time winter break arrives, things in our locker have gotten disorganized again. "It's so crowded in here!" Lara says, frustrated. Then she adds, "Maybe you should get your own locker."

I'm usually skilled at disguising emotion, but I must have shown a reaction because Lara quickly softens her tone. "I can help you find one."

"No, I agree—it is crowded," I quickly reply. I assure her I'll be out of her locker by the end of the week.

Deep down, I'm sad about the change. Lara and I have been hanging out less and less lately. The only time we've seemed to see each other these days is at our locker.

I spot an empty locker on the main floor and put my lock on it. When I go to update the office, the older admin woman says, "You don't just pick any locker. It could have been in use."

"But it wasn't," I tell her.

She gives me a stern look and says, "You're lucky that one happens to be available, but next time, ask beforehand."

Why, so you could shove me down in the damn basement again? That's what I want to say. But I don't.

The following week Lara waves me over in the hallway. "Mia!" She's excited about something.

We haven't spoken since the move.

"Let's see your new locker," she says, smiling.

As we make our way there, Lara starts telling me about one of her teachers. "He's so hot!" she adds.

I laugh.

"And he's nice to me!" she says.

"Well, of course he is…" I respond cheekily.

We both giggle. It feels good to be together.

Most students have magnetic mirrors inside their lockers, Lara included. I don't know where they bought them from or how much they cost, but my mom had a round mirror at home that detached from the plastic holder. I took it to school and taped it in my locker, along with a few clippings from a *Seventeen* magazine.

When I open my locker, Lara's eyes go straight to my makeshift "magnetic" mirror and then quickly look away.

She points at one of the magazine pictures and says, "That's cool."

After a few seconds of silence, staring into my bare locker, there is nothing left to say.

Two Paths

The last time Lara and I fought was in grade four. We don't recall what it was about, we just remember all the notes we sent back and forth.

I'm sorry.

I'm sorry too.

Can we be friends again?

Everything about our friendship was easy. We live four houses away from each other. Our birthdays are two weeks apart. Lara not only tolerated my love of rock 'n' roll music—she actually started to like it. We used to play Barbies for hours, listening to the Cars or Honeymoon Suite because they're my favorite albums.

We saw our first Saturday matinee together in sixth grade, *Pretty in Pink*. No adults! We had felt so grown-up.

And Lara got her period three months before I did. She explained everything to me, so by the time it was my turn, I didn't feel scared or embarrassed. We both developed at the same time too. We were a similar size, thank God.

Can you imagine if one of us was flat-chested? One time we even took our shirts off and stood in front of her dresser mirror and compared them.

When I moved lockers for the third time, it was really the beginning of the end of our friendship. Lara and I never verbalized our drifting apart. We had always had other friends in elementary school, yet remained best friends. But high school was so different and fast-paced—there was no time to process or keep up with the changes.

As the next few weeks, then months, passed, our attempts to remain friends started to feel forced. Awkward hellos as we passed each other in the hall, then a quick wave seemed good enough. Until the day we pretended we didn't see each other.

Lara hangs out with mostly white girls now. In the beginning, she always invited me to join them, but I wasn't interested in hanging out with her new friends.

I've been making friends with Native girls I've met through Tonya. They are a few years older than me and rarely attend school. When they do, they can be found in the smoking section by my old locker.

I don't fit in with the Native girls either, but I feel more comfortable with them than I do with Lara's friends.

The Native girls are cool. A few of them are so pretty. They have boyfriends and hang out at the video arcades. My mom gets upset when she finds out I was at the arcades. She says the reason she signed me up for so many extracurricular activities over the years was so I would stay out of arcades.

And the Native girls drink on weekends.

Lara and her white friends drink too. She had a few girls over for a sleepover and they took some booze from her dad's liquor cabinet.

By the end of eighth grade, Lara and I are no longer on speaking terms. We act like some bitter falling-out has taken place—which hasn't. In going from elementary school to high school, our friendship suddenly no longer seems to fit or make sense.

I don't think either of us expected to part ways like we did. Never would we have envisioned it. High school seemed to carve out two separate paths for us. I was assigned to the basement floor with the headbangers and smokers even though I was neither, and Lara was placed in a prime location outside the library. She went off in one direction, and I in the other. It felt like we had very little control over any of it.

Author's Note

This novel, which is based on my personal experiences growing up in Prince Rupert, is set during the 1980s.

I use terms like *Native, Native Indian* and *Indian* throughout, as that was the language used at the time. Today, *First Nations* or *Indigenous* are the appropriate words. Some of the names or spellings of Indigenous nations have changed too. I used the names that were common at the time.

When "those schools" are mentioned in the text, the characters are referring to the Indian residential schools, which were not openly talked about or widely discussed back then.

Indian residential schools operated in Canada from 1831 to 1996. Over 150,000 First Nations, Inuit and Métis children were taken from their homes and forced to attend these institutions. The abuse they suffered was horrific, and the far-reaching impacts of those atrocities are seen and felt throughout Indigenous communities to this day.

Acknowledgments

I knew if I ever wrote a book it would be dedicated to my grandmother. Mia's grandmother is based on my grandma. Just how deep and grounding her love and presence were proved hard to capture. I am forever grateful for all she did and cherish my memories growing up with her.

Thank you to my mom. Reading through the manuscript, I began to see patterns—*I went home and told my mom*. It was heartening to see how free I felt to readily share my day with you. And thank you for encouraging me to be a reader! Taking turns reading Judy Blume books aloud with you made a lasting impression.

Thank you to my extended family, which includes many cousins and aunties and uncles. We were always doing something fun. Our parents did their best to give us a good life, better than the ones they had. Thank you all so much for the love and fun times. And for your great taste in rock-and-roll music.

"Uncle Jerry" was the best, most loving uncle a child could ask for. He made everyone feel seen and special. Thank you—we all love you.

Everyone deserves a "Lara" in their life. You gently held space for me before holding space was a thing. Our friendship when we were children had such an impact on me. *Spoiler alert*—I am glad we reconnected as adults and that our friendship now is equally special. Thank you for allowing me to share our story.

When I first started writing this book, I shared the opening with a co-worker. Karai, I took your generous feedback and ran with it. Thank you.

Claudia Cornwall from The Writer's Studio at Simon Fraser University, thank you for seeing the potential in my stories. I am also appreciative of your ongoing mentorship.

My TWS cohort! The best cohort! The beautiful and sincere feedback you all provided throughout the program (many of those pieces are included in this book) meant so much.

Thank you to Cynthia Leitich Smith for your generous feedback on my manuscript.

Naomi. Even with a busy schedule, you kindly offered to read my manuscript, and your generous feedback came at such an important time and gave me a much-needed boost. Thank you so much.

Jack. The best non-agent agent around! Thanks for your mentorship, recommendation for submissions and continued guidance. You were key! I owe you a drink at the Sylvia.

My trio of an advisory panel through those last frenzied months before publication, Diana, Jade and, *wink wink,* Russ: Thank you.

So many dear family members, friends and co-workers supported and rooted for me throughout this long process. Thank you—it meant so much!

A huge thank-you to everyone at Orca Book Publishers. Ruth Linka, after our first Zoom I knew I was in good hands. A special thank-you to Jackie Lever and Tanya Trafford—you made the editing process easy for me.

And, of course, Prince Rupert. The town of my childhood. There's nowhere else like it, and it will always hold a special place in my heart.

T'oyaxsut 'nüüsm.

KIM SPENCER is a graduate of the Writer's Studio at Simon Fraser University, where she focused on creative nonfiction. Two of her short stories were published in an anthology released through SFU, and an experimental short story of hers appeared in *Filling Station* magazine. Kim was selected as a mentee by the Writers' Union of Canada for BIPOC Writers Connect, as well as for ECW's BIPOC Writers Mentorship Program. Kim is from the Ts'msyen Nation in northwest BC and currently lives in Vancouver, British Columbia.

ORCA HAS STORIES
from the heart

"A heartfelt tear-jerker about love, friendship, and courage."
—*Kirkus Reviews*

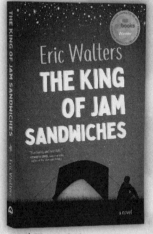

★ "Tug at the heartstrings and tickle the funny bone."
—*School Library Journal,* starred review

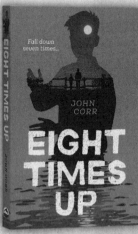

"Addressing mental health with empathy."
—*Kirkus Reviews*

"A sincere story about hope, healing, and a blooming friendship amid grief."
—*Booklist*